WRECKED

A SINGER'S GARAGE NOVEL

HELENE LAVAL

Copyright © 2021 by Helene Laval

All rights reserved.

No part of this book may be reproduced in any form or by any electronic or mechanical means, including information storage and retrieval systems, without written permission from the author, except for the use of brief quotations in a book review.

*To my friends and family for their never-ending encouragement,
and to Mallory who never let me give up.*

1

Rina

All I wanted was to get back to my car, drive home, and take a shower. I was covered in bug bites, my skin was sunburned, and my previous glistening sweat was now a sticky layer of dirt and funk.

Another tree branch whipped across my cheek as I made my way down yet another overgrown foot trail, hoping this was the one that led to the parking lot. I tucked a wisp of my light brown hair behind my ear that had broken free of my ponytail and adjusted my ball cap.

Get yourself together Rina, it's Pennsylvania for crying out loud. At worst, you'll end up on a road, or find a town. It's summer, there's water. This is ultimately survivable. You've been through worse. You want to prove to yourself you're strong. Here's your chance, I told myself as I trudged onward. I felt the sting of another branch on my cheek. *Shit.*

I leaned against a tree, rummaged in my pack for my water bottle, and took a swig of the now warm liquid. I poured a small amount on the hem of my shirt and lifted it to clean my face. Even though my cheek was stinging, there was no blood. Well, that was something. The last thing I needed was another mark on my face.

I hadn't hiked these woods since I was twelve, and that was about twelve years ago. It was the last time I was anywhere near the woods. I had good memories here, and I wanted to relive them. I thought a solitary hike would clear my mind and help give me some direction in this new life I just started. It worked too. Starting out, the sound of my footfalls thumping on the well-worn path, listening to the familiar sound of the forest, and the heaving of my own hard-earned breaths...it was amazing. The smell of sweet pine and earth, the feeling of hopping over a rushing stream, the crunch of deadfall under my feet. I loved it and felt like I could go on forever.

That was until I took a wrong turn, and my two-hour trip was now nearing five. It just all went wrong. So very, terribly, horribly wrong. Now I was over it. I just wanted to get the hell out.

It was nearly dusk when I finally stumbled off the trail and my feet landed on gravel. Gravel! The parking lot. A rush of energy surged through me. *I made it!*

I could see my car in the corner of the lot, and I started to lift my pack off my shoulder as I approached, when I noticed the rear window was busted and my car was rocking. My heart started racing, and I felt hot anger slowly rise to the surface.

I may have the oldest, crappiest car in the county, but it was *my* crappy car, and I wasn't going to let some asshole rip me off. *Oh no you don't*, I thought, slowly dropping my pack to the ground and picking up a hefty sized log at the tree-lined edge of the lot. Still moving forward, I hoisted the log over my shoulder and crept toward the car.

"I wouldn't do that if I were you." I barely registered the deep masculine voice as I turned around swinging. Before I could stop myself, I was in motion, and the log went careening into the side of a six-foot-tall man wearing a lumberjack style red and black flannel.

"Ow! What the hell?" The big guy croaked, now bent over slightly, and gripping his upper arm and side. I immediately realized what I'd done and dropped the log (it was just a really big stick, okay?) onto the pavement.

"Shit," I said. My plans of being a badass crumbled right there. My arms tingled all the way up to my shoulders and I shook them out, trying to lessen the sting. "Are you alright?" My eyes shifted from the guy to my car, which was still rocking. Some asshole was still digging through my stuff.

"I'm trying to save you a lot of grief. Do not go near that car," the big guy ground out through clenched teeth.

"That's my car. Somebody is robbing me!" I loud whispered, not wanting to give away my presence, and surely failing.

"No, that's not it. Look, just calm down, and listen to me. There's a bear trapped in that car."

I looked at him open-mouthed. "A bear?" I said in disbelief. My hands went to my hips as I waited for the guy to straighten up and explain.

"I've heard it happens, but I've never seen it. You have a black bear in your car." He stopped cradling his arm and side, and he now stood to his full height. Six feet plus tall, I'd say. Maybe more. Hard to tell when you're only 5'4" yourself.

"You have got to be kidding me." I mean, what do you say to that? I started walking toward my car to get a better look. The big guy walked right next to me. Sure enough, when I got closer to see inside the rear window, I saw a large dark shape moving around in there. Moving around *a lot*.

"What is it doing?" I asked, not turning around.

"I think it's stuck. I don't think it can get out," the man replied back.

I looked at my back window. It had a big hole in it and the glass was spiderwebbed into a thousand pieces. It was caved inward, and I could see how the animal couldn't figure its way out. I backed out of view of the car and looked around the lot. *Help?* There wasn't anybody around. There were only three cars left in the lot this late in the day. Mine, I'm assuming the lumberjack's beside me, and a passenger van with no people associated with it. They were probably in the backcountry overnight, something I've always wanted to do. That was, until today when my leisurely hike turned into a five-hour detour of misery.

I kept scanning the lot for any sort of help when my eyes locked on a sign posted right next to the nearby trash receptacle:

"Warning: Bear damage is common in this parking lot. The sight or odor of food in your vehicle greatly increases the chance of your car being damaged!"

. . .

I groaned and let my legs take me to the ground right in front of the lonely passenger van. "I will not cry, I will not cry," I repeated to myself quietly as my eyes filled with tears. I thought of the food I'd left inside, the leftover takeout from this horrible place creatively named *The Diner* down the road. The sandwich I purchased wasn't even edible, and I forgot to toss the container. I let myself be defeated. I deserved this moment. Who doesn't need a moment after something like this? "No, no, no. This can't possibly be my life," I said, staring up at the sky, trying to hold back the tears.

A pair of deep blue eyes appeared before me as the man crouched down to my level. A full head of dark hair, just long enough to curl around his ears, and an equally dark beard that looked like it hadn't been trimmed in a few days but framed a rather nice looking face. I wasn't sure I wanted him this close to me.

"Hey? Hey, are you alright?" he said to me, concern filling those pretty blue eyes. His arms rested loosely on his knees and he lifted a hand toward me. I flinched back, and startled by my reaction, he dropped it back down. I looked at him with the most determined and defiant expression I could muster at that moment and watched him study me. I saw when he recognized the faded yellow, purple, and green bruises all over my face, and comprehension dawned. *That's right, guy. Take a look, a good long look, and stay the fuck away,* I thought to myself. His eyes narrowed, and he took a deep breath, but he said nothing. I couldn't read his expression, but it wasn't pity. More like he was making a decision about something.

He stood up abruptly and said, "Okay, let's take care of this then," and walked toward the car.

I scrambled up and off the ground and chased after him. "What do you mean?"

"We're going to get it out," he said, still looking straight ahead.

"What? We can't do that, it'll eat us," I said to his hulking broad back. This guy was crazy. We couldn't possibly handle this on our own.

"It's not going to eat us," he said, still walking. He circled around, looking for something, planning something?

"How do you know that?" I followed his gaze around the lot.

"Because it's probably terrified and panicked. Not hungry."

"Terrified and panicked sounds dangerous."

"This is true." He turned to me then, appraising me up and down. "We'll have to be careful then." Smart man.

When he stopped looking around, both our gazes landed back on my car. The bear sure was making a mess in there. I could see the headrests were torn and ripped, and pieces of fabric hung from the interior roof. The bear itself wasn't making any noise but sounded like it was trying to dig its way out. I couldn't see my seats. I could only imagine.

"You see that pickup truck over there?" Mr. Tall, Dark and apparently Crazy said, pulling my attention away from my car. I looked at the big black pickup truck he was pointing at. "That's mine. You're going to wait in the cab while I let the bear out."

"The hell I am." I turned to him. I may not know this

stranger, but he seemed normal enough. A lunatic, sure, but not a serial killer type of lunatic, just an "I do dumb shit" lunatic. I didn't want him to get hurt. I didn't want that on me. No way. No fucking way.

"Look, I've never done this before, and I don't know how it's going to react. I think it will just exit the car and run off in the woods. But I don't really know. It may make a beeline for the nearest person and attack. You are safest in the truck. There's nowhere else for you to go."

"I'm not leaving you to do this on your own." He must've cued in on my solidly planted legs and lift of my chin because he didn't automatically argue with me. Point for him.

After an exasperated stroke of his messy beard, he said, "Wait here." He jogged over to his truck, got inside, and backed it up next to my car so the bed lined up close to my front door.

The bear, startled now with all the movement, became frantic. I couldn't see what it was doing, but it started making grunting noises and was whining. My car started rocking harder. *Oh shit.*

"This is what we're going to do." The guy started talking faster, like we were racing against time. Maybe we were. It sure as hell felt like it. "You're going to get in my truck while I stay in the bed. Wait, can you drive a stick shift?"

"I can." One of my mother's many boyfriends taught me when I was a teen, insisting it was an essential skill.

"Good," he continued. "When I'm in the bed, I'm going to lean over and open the car door. As soon as the door is open, you're going to pull the truck forward and away," he said quickly, again as if we had to get this done fast. I wasn't complaining. My heart was beating out of my chest. It happens when you're about to put yourself in the path of a bear.

I thought about this for about two seconds. It was more than I had in the way of a plan. "Ok, let's do it."

Within a minute, we were in place. I was at the wheel, ready to peel out as soon as that door opened. The bear was in the back seat, and I estimated we had a few seconds to get out of dodge before it torpedoed into a man-eating rampage. I watched my new friend lean out of the bed of the truck, hand reaching for my door handle. Thank goodness he was a big man. I never could've made that stretch. He looked at me in the mirror and nodded. I nodded back.

I watched him lift, tug, and swing the door ajar in a single movement. For the first time, I was grateful for the sticky spring in the door hinge, because it held itself open. As soon as most of the guy's body leaned back into the bed, I eased the clutch and rolled forward to the other end of the lot. I didn't panic and slam on the gas. It'd been a while since I drove a stick shift, and I didn't stall. I stayed calm and in control. *Go me!*

I pulled up the emergency brake, shifted in neutral, and turned around to watch. Even though the guy was all the way in the back, I could feel he was watching as intently as I was.

Nothing happened. Ten seconds later. Nothing.

I rolled down the window. "What's it doing?" I called back in my loud whisper.

"I don't know," he replied. Neither of us took our eyes off the car.

Thirty seconds of unbearable nothingness, then a cute

little nose emerged, followed by two hundred forty pounds of black bear lazily exiting my car. It was adorable. So cute and fluffy. It didn't even look in our direction. It just walked off into the woods as if he didn't have a care in the world. I watched his round furry butt slowly sway into the forest until it was out of sight. *Huh.* Well, that was a real cause for panic.

I waited another thirty seconds, then I got out of the truck. The guy hopped out of the bed. We stood next to each other and stared at my car across the lot.

"Think it's safe?" I asked, still looking straight ahead.

"I think so," he said in return.

Side by side, we walked to my car and peeked inside the open door. I let out an audible gasp. At the same time I heard a low timbered "shiiiiiiit" from my companion.

The destruction inside my vehicle was total. Every single seat cushion was unrecognizable. Foam and fabric were everywhere. The passenger door panel was completely removed, exposing the bare metal of the frame. *Shredded.* That was the term I was thinking as I looked inside my poor car.

I briefly considered driving it back home. I could pile the seat parts on top of each other and make it the ten miles down the road back to my house. Then I saw the steering wheel. As in, there wasn't one. The furry little thing ripped it off.

I sighed deeply and scrambled over what to do next. Even if there was cell phone reception, there wasn't a person in this world I could call for help. I looked around the lot and saw my pack. I walked over to it, rummaged inside, and pulled out my still half-full water bottle. I'd have to walk.

I took a drink, shrugged on my pack, and turned to the guy.

"Well, this is a first for me. I'd like to say it's been fun, but it really hasn't. Not at all. Thank you, though, for all of your help. Not to cut all this short," I waived my water bottle around the parking lot, "but I have to get going."

2

Jesse

"What do you mean you have to get going? Where? How?" I couldn't believe she was just going to take off. It made no sense. Who thinks they can just walk off to God knows where, at dusk, in the middle of nowhere?

"I can walk," the woman said as she adjusted the straps on her pack, bouncing it once to settle it in place.

"Come on. I can't just let you walk. The main road is a good five miles. Even from there, you'd have to walk eons to get anywhere."

"I can walk. I can make my way just fine."

She looked directly at me, and I saw those bruises, shades of green and yellow all over that adorable face. Old and faded bruises, but definitely there. *Not that old,* and wondered who she was, where she came from, and who the fuck hurt her. It was obvious she had something to prove and not accepting a ride from me somehow was part of it.

I took in her face. Delicate chin raised in defiance, dark brown eyes gleaming with determination. She wore a yellow trucker cap with a dark ponytail tucked through the hole. Not a stitch of makeup, but she didn't need it. Not even to cover those bruises. Her pale skin contrasted with the row of freckles across her nose and cheeks, which had gotten a nice red from the sun today. My dick stirred when I zeroed in on her plump, natural rose-colored lips. Where the hell had that come from? *Shit.* I could not go there, not with this girl. I also wasn't the type of guy that could leave a girl in the middle of nowhere, even if she asked me to. I had to help her.

I snapped out of my thoughts and said, "No, really, please let me give you a ride. I'd never be able to sleep tonight." This was true. I'm a sucker for a girl in trouble, and this one was in a heap of it.

"Thank you. Thank you for everything, truly, but I can walk," she said, and started to pass me heading toward the road, the gravel crunching beneath her feet.

"No, you can't!" I raised my voice. *Fuck.* I had to be careful about that. I have a deep voice, and I've been told it sounds scary when I'm angry. She didn't jump, but I saw the startled look she gave me. I took a deep breath and stepped back, giving her space.

"Come on, honest, I'm a nice guy." I lifted my hands in surrender.

"You don't look like a nice guy."

Really? Now I was starting to get offended. I knew I didn't look my best at the moment, but hadn't my actions just proved I wasn't a danger? And I wasn't *that* scruffy, I didn't have a mountain man beard or anything.

"I just helped you get a *bear* out of your car. Is that not a nice thing? And if I don't look like a nice guy, what do I look like then?"

She looked me over, and I think she actually sniffed the air.

"A not nice guy. Kind of scary."

"Lady, I just spent three nights in the backcountry and hiked twenty-seven miles. We all look like this when we emerge from the forest. That's why we go. No grooming required." This was ridiculous.

"Alright, you may not be at your best," she relented. "But you kind of look like the bear that was trapped in my car."

I took a deep breath, brushed off the insult, and tried to think. *Infuriating.* No way. There was no way on earth I could leave this girl alone up here in this parking lot.

I mentally ran through some options. I could make a run at her and throw her in my truck. No, that sounded really bad, even in my own head. Why did I just think of going all kidnapper? We'd probably crash at her desperate need to escape. One look at her and I knew I couldn't trap her in my truck like that poor bear. She'd tear *me* to shreds.

"Look, if you don't want to get in the truck with me, how about I let you drive? I'll sit in the bed of the truck. That way I feel manly and helpful and not like a jerk. You'll feel safe and in control." There. That was reasonable. Right? Crazy maybe, and not something I would usually consider, but it was doable.

She thought about this for way longer than she needed to.

I saw her mind weighing her options, finally coming to the conclusion that this was acceptable and realizing it was the only way I'd leave her alone.

"Ok. That'll work."

3

Rina

After having my car mauled by a bear in the parking lot (A freaking *bear*—I'm not about to get over this anytime soon!), I'm "rescued" by Paul Bunyan. The man was big. In lieu of lumberjack jeans, he wore tan hiking pants and a good pair of leather boots. But with the flannel, I half expected an axe slung over his shoulder.

What choice did I have? Really. The more he talked, the more dire my situation looked. I was pretty near certain I would've never made it back to the house by daybreak, and it was nearly dark now. Somebody would find my half-frozen body by the side of the road in the morning. It was summer, but I was beginning to feel the chill now that I'd stopped walking and the adrenaline rush from the bear had faded. I wasn't dressed for spending a night in the forest. Summer or not.

The lumberjack hopped into the bed of the truck. Literally hopped over one-handed with admirable ease, and I couldn't help but appreciate his lean muscular frame and fine ass in those pants. Once he shifted a few things around, I'm assuming his pack and whatever men like him had in the bed of their trucks, he settled in against the cab and said, "My name is Jesse. I'm assuming the keys are still inside. Where are you taking me?"

I opened the driver's door and climbed in. Should I introduce myself? The guy was trusting me with his life and saving mine all at the same time. Before I shut the door, I leaned out and said, "I'm Rina, and I'm headed down to Song."

Once inside, I adjusted the seat, took a deep breath, pressed on the clutch, and turned over the engine. I smoothly transitioned into first gear and pulled out on the road. Once we were on the move, I heard the back window slide over. "Hey!" I yelped in surprise.

"Sorry, sorry...I thought I should at least be within shouting distance." Once I realized there was no way a man of that size was squeezing through that back window, I relaxed.

"Song, huh? That's where I live. It's not a big place; we probably aren't far from each other. I've not seen you around before."

I didn't say anything. I didn't know what to say. I didn't really want anybody to know my business. Plus, was I supposed to have a screaming conversation with this guy through a truck window? Finally, I just yelled back, "Sorry, I can't really hear you. I'm only about ten minutes from here."

A few minutes later, we landed in town. Song, Pennsylvania, was nestled in the eastern foothills of the Pocono Mountains. It was a rundown reminder of days gone by, but while local factories and mines faded out, roads to the nearby lakes attracted more and more visitors seeking weekend escapes from the city. Song was right on that pathway; it just didn't realize it yet.

I always loved the name, Song. Despite Pennsylvania being known for some pretty bizarrely named towns, including the snort-worthy Intercourse, Blue Ball, and Climax, Song always felt good to my ears. The town was not very big, so I settled on driving down to The Diner, which will be on my shit list for the rest of my life. I didn't want to take Jesse to the house, my house, and let him know where I was staying. Not to mention there was nobody there, and the houses were far enough apart that I doubted anyone would hear me if Jesse turned out to be a bad guy.

The Diner was a fifteen-minute walk, and I would be able to handle that just fine. I pulled into the lot, and Jesse jumped out before I could park the break. I jumped when his face appeared in the driver's side window. He had a big handsome smile but dropped it the instant he saw my surprised reaction. I leaned back, and he quickly stepped back, obviously giving me space. He relaxed into an easygoing stance and placed his hands in his pockets. I appreciated that. Maybe he wasn't a "Not nice guy" after all.

4

Jesse

After my conversation failed through the back window, I kept quiet. On the drive, I let my mind wander about the woman driving my truck. Who was she? She was obviously cautious around people. Despite her skittishness and caution, she had that *keep far away* vibe that told me to do just that or the claws were coming out. Hence me getting walloped by a branch up in the parking lot. She was reactive for reasons I didn't know. I had to respect that and try to be on my best behavior. She pulled into The Diner, which had the worst food for a hundred miles. I jumped out of the truck bed and walked to the driver's window. I was smiling, but one look at her face and I knew it was time to back off again, so I did. She turned off the engine. I saw her lean over for her pack and slide out of the truck with an easy grace in time with the door opening.

She looked around the lot before she spoke. "I can walk from here."

She seemed more at ease than earlier. Damn, she was beautiful. She was short, but not tiny. Wearing a pair of shorts and a tank top that showed off toned legs and arms, she was also soft and curvy at the same time. Her tank top hugged perfectly sized breasts that I suddenly had the desire to put my hands on.

"Hello?" I heard her say, and I don't think it was the first time. Shit. I realized I was staring. *I am such a dick.* I shook out of it and looked her in the eyes. As soon as we locked eyes, she tossed the keys at me. Quick and accurate, I caught them easily. She hoisted her pack onto her shoulders and adjusted her shirt hem around it. When she looked up again, she said, "Um, look, I'm actually really grateful that you came along when you did. You know, I might have gotten eaten. And also, the ride. It was pretty stupid of me to think I could walk. I don't know how I would've made it back."

I harrumphed. "They would've found you frozen on the side of the road come morning." She stared at me like I had two heads, then a barely there smirk lifted one side of her mouth.

"I had that same thought. I didn't bring a sweatshirt." She looped her thumbs through the shoulder straps and looked around the lot again before her eyes landed back on me.

"Well, anyway, thank you, Jesse. Like I said, I can walk from here, I'm not far. Although I'm starting to believe you are a nice guy after all, I'm good to go."

"No way." I was dumbfounded. Not this shit again. "Look, I already told you I can't let you walk home. That would be really awful of me, and not very manly or chivalrous."

"Seriously, thank you. You've already been plenty chivalrous. I'm only a ten or twenty-minute walk. No hard feelings, but I don't know you at all, and I don't want you to know where I live."

That I could understand, but my blood was starting to boil. Really? Haven't I shown that I'm a decent person? I am not somebody that lets a woman walk home in the dark and just be okay with it. But something told me I would not, under any circumstances, win this argument. She looked like she was preparing to run if she had to, just to get away from me. I had to come up with a solution for this one, and fast.

"I tell you what, got a cell phone?" I asked.

"Yeah?" she answered, skeptical.

"Look, I can respect there is no way you are letting me take you to your home. But I'm going to beg for you to send me a text when you're safe inside. Would you do that? If I don't know you got home safe, it'll seriously ruin my week. And I have a lot to do and concentrate on this week. I can't be thinking about a beautiful woman wandering the roads, possibly in a ditch somewhere. Would you do that? I'd consider it a thank you for the lift down the hill. And the bear."

I noticed her tilt her head when I called her beautiful, but her frown never lifted. She stared at me for a moment, a contemplative stare, and shrugged off her pack and rummaged around. I felt like a pathetic ass and a fool as I waited for her to emerge with a cell phone. She held it in two hands like a precious bird. As the screen lit up and she rocked back on her heels, she looked up at me and asked, "Okay, what's your number?"

I let out a huge breath of relief and let a smile spread across my face. I rattled the number off as she typed it in.

"Thank you again, Jesse. For everything."

She turned and started out of the lot. I watched her go, all determined pride and confidence.

5

Rina

The poor guy was rambling on and on, I couldn't stand it. I didn't want to keep arguing with him, because I really wanted to go home. If I was honest with myself, he was every bit a gentleman, which made him more adorable and simultaneously handsome by the minute.

"Okay, what's your number?" I asked.

He let loose an enormous, relieved, genuine smile that lit up his face and reached all the way to those lovely eyes. It was so disarming, it took all my concentration to type it in and not focus on his beautiful face. Twenty minutes ago, this guy was a stranger, and now? Now I felt that I'd known him forever.

Hoping he didn't see my reaction and my fingers shake, I gathered up as much confidence as I could, and walked away like I'd done it a million times before.

As I walked, I thought about this evening and my actions. The logical side of my brain told me there were more good guys in the world than bad guys, but the last five years had me confused. I only left Brad ten days ago. Ten days without that asshole, and the remnants of bruising on my face reminded me every morning what could happen when I trusted somebody, what I never wanted to happen again, and why I was here in the first place. I was here to be a normal person, so I should act normal and reasonable. I would not let Brad turn me into a scared, fragile victim. Did I hate the guy? You bet. But I hated myself more for getting into the situation in the first place.

I found out Brad had taken my mail, and with it, a notice that my grandfather died. He never said a word. Four months ago. Grandpa died *four months* ago. I missed the funeral. He was buried alone, without ceremony. I would never forgive myself for that. It wasn't until nearly two weeks ago when a lawyer came to our loft in the city. Brad was at work and explained that he had been trying to contact me for months. He told me everything about my grandfather's passing (heart attack) and as the executor of his will, he informed me I was now the owner of grandpa's small cape cod home. Along with the keys to the house, he handed me a check.

I sat frozen and sick to my stomach on the edge of the sofa for what seemed like hours after the lawyer left. Eventually, I wiped enough tears away and packed my clothing. I left all of the fancy dresses and shoes behind. I looked around me and realized I'd been in a prison.

My mother and I had lived with Grandpa for several years. Life was good then, the best it ever was. Until one day when I was thirteen, my mother told me she met a man, and we were moving to the city. I cried and screamed, but she dragged me away from Grandpa and the life I loved. A few years after that, she found herself a new man, and when I was eighteen, left me to fend for myself. She told me Grandpa didn't ever want to see us again. That he'd disowned us and to forget about him. With Mom gone, I was struggling just to make ends meet, trying to stay in college, but I wasn't going to make it. And then I met him.

He was handsome, charming, and being fifteen years older, seemed so mature and worldly and like he had everything. It was a fast romance, and I quickly moved in with him. He said he'd take care of me, and he did.

I'm pretty sure I was traumatized by my mother leaving me. I never imagined that she'd take off as she did. But there it was. At the moment, I wanted somebody to care for me and I'm sure Brad saw it too. I had some friends from school I used to hang out with, but Brad would get upset or jealous. Not enraged or anything, just little comments to make me feel guilty, so I stopped hanging out with them. At the end of my first and only semester of school, Brad thought I should take some time off. According to him, I was traumatized and needed time to heal. I even left my part-time job at the coffee shop, which I loved. He didn't let me worry. He paid all the bills and took care of me, and I was grateful.

Slowly, things got worse. He tracked my phone and questioned why I took so much time at the grocery. I didn't see my life getting taken from me, bit by bit, until I literally had nothing left. Not until that lawyer showed up at my door did I see so clearly where I ended up. The anxiety I lived with every single day, in fear I did something wrong.

Brad came home and saw my bag by the door. I immediately confronted him and what he had done. I told him I was leaving. He grabbed me by the shoulders and told me to calm down, that we would go together. I said no, that I was leaving. He stood in front of the door and tried to block me. I tried to move around him.

That's when he started to beat me. I didn't see it coming. He had never so much as lifted a finger to me before. I was in such shock, I didn't even have the wherewithal to fight back at first. When a neighbor knocked on the door, I took that as my chance to run.

I hid at a local hotel for a week, trying to figure out what to do. I was alone, and I was scared to be alone. I was embarrassed that I not only was a victim, but I *looked* like a victim. I did a lot of soul searching during those days. The truth was, I spent all this time in fear of being alone, in fear of being unloved and abandoned, only to realize I had been all of those things all along. I promised myself that I would never, ever find myself in that position again.

The money my grandfather left me wasn't much, just a few thousand dollars. But it was enough to get myself a cheap car, a prepaid cell phone, and maybe if I was careful, enough to start a new life. Once I felt my bruises had healed enough to face the world, I made my way to Song.

I had a new start. When I watched Jesse study the bruises on my face, I decided I would not cower or be afraid. I would be strong and rise above my victim status.

Jesse, this stranger that appeared out of nowhere and rescued me from a bear (a bear!). I pictured the huge, relieved grin on his face when I told him to give me his number. He had an easy-going demeanor, and I believe was genuinely trying to be helpful, but I was just too rattled to take it in. I mentally scolded myself. Men and relationships had absolutely no place in my life. Not now, and I wasn't sure, if ever.

6

Rina

Grandpa's house, no *my house*, really was a fifteen-minute walk. The house was small and cottage-like, with a nice big front porch and two enormous maple trees in the front yard. Backed up to and nestled in forested land, as many Pennsylvanian homes were, it sat on a sparsely populated road. The closest house was a good five hundred yards away. I was near the end of the dead end road. It was neglected and run down, but I loved it.

When I arrived only last week, I balked at the amount of work that needed to be done, but it was mostly elbow grease and cosmetics, and I'd been chipping away at tidying it up. The first night here, I had no electricity, and I slept on the old worn sofa. I didn't know where anything had been kept, so I used the light from my phone, praying it wouldn't run the battery down, and crashed. In the morning, I made a few phone calls to get the utilities turned on, and by the end of the day, I was in business.

Despite the hike, the trauma of the bear and car incident, and my adventure getting home, I wasn't all that tired when I got back, but I was hungry. I only had a few essentials, meaning to stock up later. I heated up leftover pizza from the night before and went over my mental to-do list. I would have to call a garage and find a tow first thing in the morning. I suppose I could afford to rent a car for a day or two, but that wouldn't get me far. The most important thing was to find a job, especially now that I didn't have a car. I hadn't even started looking, thinking I'd have some time to get settled in and let the very last of the bruises heal. The cash I had was burning fast, and if I wanted to make it on my own and even make some repairs to this place, I'd need a job.

Washing my dish in the sink, my mind wandered to Jesse again. I could barely wrap my brain around the day's events, but something about Jesse and that beautiful smile of his made my chest squeeze tight. I thought of how nice his ass hugged his hiking pants, and my thighs squeezed tight too. *What? No way.* I cannot believe my mind was going there! *No. No. No!* I scolded myself. I needed to stay away from men, for crying out loud. The guy was kind, and I appreciated his caution around me. I fished out my phone from the hall where I left it. I owed the guy a text.

Me: Home. Thank you.

I waited for a response. Why was I anxious? I couldn't say. Was I excited to get a response? No. Definitely no.

Jesse: Glad to know I can sleep tonight. You're welcome.

I found myself smiling down at the screen. *Shit.* I decided I better get to bed before my mind wandered off again. I had a long day ahead. New life and all that. I hope I didn't dream about lumberjacks.

When I woke in the morning, I Googled some local towing companies. Singer's Garage was the closest place by a long shot. Singer's Garage in Song, PA. It made me smile. I explained the situation to the guy on the other end of the line—where my car was, and what happened to it.

"Let me get this straight, a bear got trapped in your car, and destroyed it?" Disbelief and laughter in his voice.

I huffed out a long sigh, "Yes, I believe I told you this twice now. This is not a prank. I left some food inside, and the bear must've really liked The Diner's Italian Hoagie. I don't know how. It wasn't edible for a human, which is why it was still in the takeout box in the car."

The guy on the line barked out a laugh. "The Diner? They have the worst food ever."

"No kidding. Now, can you tow my car and take a look at the damage for me or not?"

"Sure, my brother's out on a call, but I'll put it in the queue for the day." He continued to ramble, "Oh man, I can't wait to tell him about this." The guy chuckled over the phone. "That's one of his favorite spots, ya know. If a bear had done that to his truck, I think he would come back wearing a bear cape like a mountain man." He laughed again and then said, "Give me your name and number and we'll give you a call when we get it down here and assess the damage."

I gave him the info and thanked him for getting to it today. With nothing more to do than sit around and wait, I decided I'd head into town and grab a few cleaning supplies and groceries. I didn't have a car. The house didn't have a garage, just a small parking area next to the house, but there was a shed in the backyard. I had daydreams of seeing a bright and shiny bike back there, but sadly there was nothing of the sort, just some more junk for me to clean up. Damn, Grandpa was a hoarder. And I wondered what happened to his car? Did he even have a car? If he did, it wasn't here and couldn't help me anyway.

I walked this stretch last night, I could do it again. I shrugged on the old pack I used yesterday, another of Grandpa's stash of strange items, and walked into town.

I wouldn't exactly call the town quaint, but it had potential. With a little love and a group of motivated folks, it could be a really lovely spot. It was on the main route toward the lake, so it did have its fair amount of traffic coming through. You could practically see the hopeful looks on travelers' faces, looking for a decent place to stop. A local favorite like, "The best place for pie, or meatballs, or whatever" but sadly, there wasn't much. Two fast-food chain restaurants, and a Main Street which had more closed storefronts than open ones. There was also a chain grocery, and a local mom and pop grocery on the sparse end that I had no idea how they stayed in business. I headed for the mom and pop place called creatively, "Grocer." On my way down the empty sidewalk, I noticed an artfully decorative sign titled, "Betsy's Coffee." It had classic black-and-white striped awnings, and two small tables and chairs on the sidewalk. It occupied just a sliver of Main Street but was by far the nicest shop on the street.

I peeked inside and decided I would really love a cup of coffee. I hesitated as the familiar sense that I was doing something wrong whooshed through my brain. I reminded myself that yes, I am a grown woman and can make my own decisions. I can have a cup of coffee; I even have my own money. I don't have to turn in a receipt for this purchase. Yes, Brad had me bring a receipt of everything I bought. He would never approve of this. That he would let me go to the grocery at all really was for his own selfishness, and his only concession. Once again, I berated myself for being so stupid. It seemed so normal at the time. How did I not see it?

I shook myself out of those thoughts, steeled my shoulders, opened the door, and let myself soak in the divine smell of delicious, heavenly coffee. My mouth watered when I entered.

"Hi, hon, what can I get ya?" A beautiful woman greeted me with a friendly smile. She was in her late thirties, and average height with dark shoulder-length hair tied up in a red ribbon. With her cream-colored skin and ruby red lips, she looked like Snow White, or some long past actress from the 1940s, exuding class and confidence. She wore a blue apron over her cropped jeans and a white short-sleeved button-down shirt. She leaned over the counter smiling, as I looked at the chalkboard menu behind her.

"Hi." I smiled back. Besides that Jesse guy last night, and the garage guy this morning, this woman was the first friendly person I talked to in a week, and I instantly liked her.

"What's your favorite?" I asked. She tilted her head, still smiling. It was apparent she was waiting for more.

I cleared my throat, "When I worked in a coffee shop, I loved when customers asked me that. I'd make up something fabulous for them." She gave me an uncertain look and then replied, "Ohhh-kay, challenge accepted. This is at your own risk," she said with a wink and set about making me a coffee.

In just a few short minutes, she placed a steaming cup of coffee on the counter with a big frothy top sprinkled with cinnamon. It was a work of art.

"This looks heavenly." I smiled at her. "Thank you." I paid for my mystery coffee and sat down at one of the empty tables near the window, while the barista helped other customers. I spent a few minutes watching people walk up and down the street while I drank my coffee, which tasted every bit as good as it looked.

I loved just sitting without a time limit or worry. I didn't realize how stressful my life had been before. How every little thing made me anxious. I had become incapable of making a single decision without approval. I felt the familiar anger rising up again. I really enjoyed being a barista, and I wondered if this place was hiring. I made a mental note to ask before I left. That anger and shame filled me up inside and I felt the tears starting to well. I looked around and took a deep breath, not letting them escape, and smiled at the barista who was cleaning up vacated tables.

She finished her task and sat down in the chair opposite me, eyes gleaming. "So you wouldn't happen to be looking to work in a coffee shop again, would you?"

"Are you reading my mind? I walked into town to find a job today." I could imagine the stunned look on my face, but I'm sure there was a smile breaking free somewhere.

She reached across the table and held out her hand. "I'm

Betsy Reed. One of my baristas is leaving for school in about two weeks and wants to take some time off before then. 'Summer of Fun' or whatever." She rolled her eyes and lifted both hands while saying "whatever."

"What do you say?" she asked with a genuine smile. "I don't even know if what you said about working in a coffee shop is true or not, but I really need to find new help, and experience matters." She gave me a cross between a grimace and a smile, as if she felt she stepped over the line, but was still hoping for the best,

"Seriously?" I asked.

She nodded back at me.

"You're not going to believe this. I just moved here this week. And yes, I needed a job yesterday."

Betsy didn't ask many questions. I think she felt that same sense of friendship in me as I did her. We worked out a schedule and I, bursting with newfound energy, bounded down to the grocery to grab a few essentials, then walked home with a smile on my face. My life back indeed! One step at a time and a job did a whole lot to ease my fears. Things were looking up.

7

Jesse

It's true that crazy things happen during a full moon, as last night was. I spent the morning running from pick up to pick up. So much for being slow. The rare opportunity I had to take off in the mountains for a few days was a distant memory. Was that really just yesterday? The garage was quickly filling up, and with each new client, I could see my restoration projects getting pushed farther and farther back. Yes, I had a good business, and we had a good reputation. I had a talented crew of mechanics and we'd get the job done. But I made some good additional cash on restorations. Jameson was headed into his last year of school and after that, I'd be in really good shape.

I pulled into the lot and started unloading a 2006 Chevy pickup that decided not to turn over for its owner this morning when Jameson caught up with me.

"Jesse, you have a pick up off of Parson's Road, at the lake trailhead. Get this, some woman called, and her car got destroyed by *a bear*." He leaned back on his heels, his arms crossed over his chest, a big shit-eating grin on his face.

We were about the same 6'2" with a similar build, but where I currently had shaggy dark hair and a close-cropped beard, Jameson inherited more of the Irish side, with reddish-brown hair and a slightly lighter complexion. He was seven years younger than me and was your typical all-American college boy. I walked over to unhook the chains underneath the truck and casually said, "Yeah, I know the car. I gave the girl a ride last night."

"You what? How did you not tell me this morning?" His voice and expression was incredulous.

"I didn't think about it, okay? The phone started ringing the second I got in and I've been on the move before your lazy ass decided to make an appearance today."

"Tell me about the car. Oh man, I've heard of this happening, but I've never seen it. Did you see the bear too?"

"I did. It was in her car. I helped free it."

"Dude. No shit. That's crazy."

"I never saw anything like it. It might be a total loss. Who knew that a bear could do that much damage?" I had indeed thought fleetingly about the incident several times today, but I was just too busy. If I thought more on it, I would've realized we were going to be getting that car this morning, being the only tow for miles.

"Tell me more, Brother, this is the best story of the week. Maybe of my whole summer. I can't wait to take pictures. I looked this up on YouTube to make sure the girl wasn't pulling my leg. Sure enough. It happens." He started laughing again. "I gotta see this—wait, you said you gave the woman a ride? Who was she? Didn't she run away from you in fear? Oh man, you probably looked like a scary as shit motherfucker walking out of the forest. I know how you get, all unwashed and primal like."

"Fuck off," I said with a smile. "I did sort of terrify her. So I let her drive my truck and I rode home in the bed of the truck."

"You let her drive your truck? You're shitting me." He stared at me open mouthed. "You won't even let me drive your truck. What the fuck, man?" He punched me in the shoulder.

"It was dark, she was alone, and I spooked her. I couldn't leave her. I left her at The Diner. She wanted to walk from there. Understandable. She even texted me when she got home. I made her promise."

"Jesse, you are too good a man," Jameson said, smiling and shaking his head. "Always saving somebody. No wonder the ladies are chasing you all over the place."

He said it, not me. I couldn't stand it. All the ladies that chased me wanted something I wasn't willing to give. A car, some money, somebody to take care of them. They never actually cared about me. They thought they could just suck my dick and I'd be happy forever and keep buying them shit. Maybe it was because nice guys do finish last, but I thought it was more because we lived in a depressed area without many options out there for most. Not that blow jobs don't make me happy; they absolutely do. Just for once I'd like to not feel like everything had a price. I was done with that shit forever after the stunt with my last girlfriend.

And right on cue, an old electric blue firebird pulled into the lot. I mentally groaned.

"And that is exactly what I'm talking about." Jameson slapped me on the back. "This one is all yours," he said, walking away smirking.

The door swung open and a pair of long, lean legs wearing a set of too-high black heels slid out of the car, followed by a nice looking woman, with too little clothing on for mid-afternoon.

"Jesse. I'm so glad you're here!" Teresa DiCarlo said as she straightened out her clothes walking toward me. "My car is making a clicking sound when I turn. Can you take a look?"

"Hi, Teresa. I've told you before, you can make an appointment and drop your car off." I did not have time for this shit.

She walked swiftly towards me, and I nearly eye rolled at the desperation. I backed up a few steps, and she moved faster. She was wearing a black mini skirt, a red scoop top that was too low, her cleavage about to spill over, and too shiny lip gloss smeared across thin lips. At first glance you'd check her out, like seeing a porn star on the street. At second glance, you'd see the fine lines indicating she was a decade older than you thought, signs of a hard life and harder men. She oozed desperation that even a sucker like me knew to stay far away from. It's a shame too because Teresa could be a beautiful woman, if she dressed like one and had more self-confidence.

"It just needs a quick look see. Let's just take it for a drive around the block, and I'll show you." She sidled up to me, way closer than I liked. "I'd like to show you."

I helped her out once. Just once. She has a couple little kids about eight and six. Stranded on the side of the road, I saw her helpless, kids playing in the dirt, Teresa on her phone trying to find somebody to contact. I just happened to drive by in my tow truck and towed her and her kids back to the garage and replaced her battery free of charge. I felt bad for her, and I felt bad for the poor kids. To have a momma like this. Hanging onto the one car she owned since high school, when her family had better times. I didn't touch her. No way would I touch her. I was just being nice, and she was in tears about not having the money for the battery, let alone a tow. So I went pro bono, trying to do the right thing. Since then she's been hounding me. I kept thwarting her attempts at trying to "pay me back" and now it had come to this. Maybe she was hard up for a lay, but I'm thinking it's more hard up for cash. Or maybe a baby daddy.

"Sorry, Teresa, I have a car to pick up." I hoisted myself into the cab of the tow truck. With a wave, I said, "Call the garage, make an appointment," and left her pouting in the lot.

I called Jameson on my cell as I pulled out. "I'm headed up to get the bear car."

"Are you sure it was a bear?"

"I told you I saw it with my own damn eyes."

"You did, you did, but I still can't believe it, man. I still can't believe it."

"It was no big deal. Really. I'll head up there now, be back soon." I hung up before Jameson could keep yammering.

The windy and heavily wooded drive up Parson's road brought back yesterday with the woman, Rina. She was adorable. Not a stitch of makeup, a normal jeans and T-shirt kind of girl. Not at all like the girls I tend to see around, and I liked it. Most of the women I came across these days were at the bar, fishing for a one nighter, or more than I bargained for. Although I understood her not wanting to show me where she lived, I saw she was independent and could handle things on her own. I needed more women like that in my life and I wanted to know more about her.

What luck that she called Singer's? Well, not really, we were the only place for miles. It looked like I was going to get my chance to see her again, and the thought made my dick twitch.

I made my way up to the trailhead parking lot, and the car was right where we left it. There wasn't anybody around, thank goodness, I was sick of explaining this already. I didn't want to deal with any park rangers either. Those guys could be assholes. I chuckled to myself thinking that might be Jameson one day. He loved the outdoors as much as I, and nearly having completed his degree in forestry, chances were good that's exactly what he'd end up doing.

I did feel bad for the poor bear though. I can't imagine the stress it went through trapped like it was. As I got closer to hook up the chains to slide the car on the bed, an awful smell hit me, and it was coming from the car.

"Oh my God." I gasped and covered my nose. The acrid smell burned my eyes. Of course, the bear shit and pissed in the car. Combine the fact that it was probably stressed out of its mind and a morning full of summer heat, and there you have it. The worst smell in the world. I hooked up and secured it as fast as I could and towed the car back to the shop.

Jameson was in the lot when I arrived back, along with my body man, Steve. I rolled down the window and leaned my head out. "Steve, it's your day off, why are you here?"

Steve joined Singer's from Texas about a year ago, and seamlessly fit into our garage family. Just an inch or so shorter than me and a slightly leaner build, Steve's dark, tanned skin and short, cropped black hair showed his Latin heritage. He was a shameless flirt, funny, always in a good mood, and apparently had a smile that melted panties off women.

"Are you kidding? I'm not missing this. Jameson called and told me you got a car that was mauled by a bear. I was headed down to O'Dell's anyway, so stopped by."

O'Dell's was our local bar, and our favorite hangout. The usual rough around the edges, but makes a decent sandwich type of place, and has a good selection of beer on tap. I think Steve had a thing for the bartender, Annie, who wouldn't give him the time of day, but explained why he was headed to the bar in the early afternoon.

I backed up to unload the car. I heard the guys gawking and saying things like, "Holy shit, do you think that's a claw mark?" I jumped out of the car and spoke over to Jameson, "Hey Jay, can you unhook that front chain?"

He jumped up alongside the car to do just that, when I heard a, "Holy fuck! What is that?" Then I heard a retching and gagging sound on the other side of the vehicle.

I walked around and saw Jameson leaning over, hands on his thighs. His face was beet red, and he was gasping. Damn kid could never handle anything putrid. Steve burst out laughing and so did I. "Is that piss and shit?" asked Steve. Jameson made another gagging sound.

"Yup," I said. I was certain there was no hope for this car. Poor girl, I hope she had insurance.

8

Rina

I spoke to the young man at the garage. He was still polite, but when he told me about the severe damage to my car, he was distinctly "off." Like even mentioning the damage caused him physical pain.

"Are you sure it's a total loss?"

"Well, no, but the repairs will most definitely be more than the car is worth. Plus, um, there is a matter of the cleanup."

"What cleanup?"

"Well, um, it appears the animal urinated and defecated inside the vehicle. And well, for lack of a better explanation, it's the grossest smell I've ever been around."

"Seriously?" I asked.

"Yes ma'am," the kid said on the other end of the phone, ending with an uncomfortable cough.

"You're telling me that not only did a bear get trapped in my car and tore it to pieces, but also crapped inside it?"

"And urinated too."

"Good grief. What do I do then?"

"Well, we could scrap it for you, and you'd at least get some cash for it. You'd have to come by and sign some paperwork for us."

"I'll have to think about that. I mean, I'll do it, but need a few minutes to take all this in. What are your office hours?"

The man I'd been speaking to, Jameson, he said his name was, told me the garage hours and said to come by any time.

Well, shit. I expected my car to be bad, but from what this man was saying, it was *really* bad. What was I going to do now? I had a job, but there was no way I could afford another car.

I stared around Grandpa's house. The place was a wreck. It wasn't "dirty," it just had a lot of clutter, and still had that stale feeling houses get when they've been empty for a while, and with Grandpa gone four going on five months ago now, it felt like a tomb. The house was a lot like my life. It had potential—all it needed was a good cleaning, decluttering, and some minor repairs.

It was time to stop wallowing in my own self-pity. My life wasn't going to fix itself. It was time to figure a few things out.

9

Jesse

Later that evening, I met up with my guys at O'Dell's for a few beers and to unwind from the hectic day. O'Dell's was your average small town bar. It had bare brick walls with a large, mirrored bar along one side. A dozen or so tables and booths spread throughout, a pair of pool tables, and four dart boards toward the back. The music was moderately loud via jukebox, but a small stage area was set up for live music. The food was decent, and during the week, it was a steady business of the local blue collar variety. On the weekends, live music drew a livelier and younger crowd. Song was a working town, with a few folks trying to improve its appeal to the touristy outsiders. Annie O'Dell was tall, lean, and pretty, with short cropped blonde hair and a heart-shaped face and was the owner and bartender. She worked long days and longer nights, but her efforts at introducing live music and a decent lunch menu were definite improvements on what once was a local bike bar.

My crew, Steve, Michael and Jameson, were already seated at the long side of the bar when I sidled up beside them. Annie, gave me a chin tilt over the music, poured, then leaned over to give me my usual beer.

"Good night, Annie?" I asked.

"Now that you're here, Jesse," she said with a wink, and off she went to help another customer. Annie kept to herself. She didn't smile at everybody and was often all business. She was fierce when it came to her bar and the good people in it. Local folks did not mess with her. It was rumored she had a shotgun under that bar. If that were true, I'd never doubt she'd use it. Annie's father was serving a fifteen year prison sentence for gun related charges. Even though he was locked up, Big Jim O'Dell, the former president of the Death Angel's MC, still had people looking after his little girl. Nobody fucked with Annie. Ever.

I found Jameson, animated as usual, excitedly telling a story. The guys were in the midst of laughter as I approached.

"And the smell. Man, it was the worst thing I've ever experienced. Worse than the time Leslie Halloway blew chunks all over me at the Halloween Bash in eleventh grade," Jameson rattled on, eyes gleaming.

"The year you blew chunks right back at her, isn't that right, Jay?" I said as I walked up to him with a slap on the back.

"Fuck off, I have a weak stomach for shit like that. You should know this," Jameson said to me as I dodged a chuff on the shoulder.

"Oh, I know it. I grew up with you, remember? Remember

the one and only time Mom asked you to clean dog shit out of the front yard for the neighbor?"

"Seriously, man, why you gotta razz me so hard? I'm trying to tell a story here," Jameson whined.

"That bad?"

This from Michael, my tech genius mechanic. He was as tall as me, but broader and menacing. Short blonde hair, slightly long on top with a well maintained dark blond beard. I've heard women refer to him as "The Viking," and it was spot on. Michael said as few words as possible in any situation, disappeared sometimes without a sound, and was the only one of us who hadn't seen the disaster yet. We all nodded solemnly in unison. Steve then started making a retching sound, and all of us busted out into laughter again.

"Fuck off," Jameson said, still smiling. "Fuck the fuck off."

"Oh by the way, Jesse, I talked to the owner, Rina Sullivan. She just moved here. I think she was in shock. The car is a loss. She doesn't have anything but liability, and it wouldn't be worth the fix. She's going to stop by and sign papers for us to scrap it."

"When?" I asked, a little too quickly, and my smart as shit brother smirked at my sudden interest.

"Didn't say. But seeing how you just lit up, she must be hot. Damn, you look dreamy." He elbowed me in the side and egged me on with his eyebrows.

"Shut up, Jay, she's just a girl. No, a woman. Reserved, and not too friendly. She didn't say much, and she wasn't very trusting." My mind wandered, thinking about her in that yellow cap with those cute as hell freckles on her nose. Then I remembered the bruises. I didn't want to say anything to the guys about it, but I had a fierce impulse to protect her.

Instead, I said, "So, be nice to her when she does stop by, okay? Don't want to scare her out of town with your blustery and forceful personality."

"You mean my charming boyish good looks," Jameson said.

"No, I mean your dumb college frat boy thing. It's too pushy."

"Better than your scary as hell axe murderer look you have going on," he said, stroking one hand down his jaw and gesturing at my beard.

"Hey, I trimmed it. It looks good," I said, defensive.

"It does, it does," Jameson admitted.

"Look who just walked in." Steve interrupted our banter while looking at the door. "Shit, Jesse you're in trouble." This time Steve took a shot at my bicep, smiling.

I looked over toward the door and eyed my ex-girlfriend, Mandy. She strode through the bar flanked on either side by Kimberlee, "make sure you know how to spell it," and Gina "I'll be a hanger-on the rest of my life." The two sidekicks had been stuck to Mandy like glue for as long as I've known them. All three wore too tight dresses, too much makeup, and too much entitlement.

Mandy and I had ended things permanently six months ago. Things went south, so far south that there wasn't a chance in hell I'd consider touching her ever again. She still couldn't take no for an answer. She made it clear she only wanted money, and maybe my dick. Money and a lot of other guys dicks too. She fucked me over so badly, and in one of the worst ways possible—it disgusted me to even look at her. Mandy was beautiful, there was no denying that. Long blonde hair, legs for days, and at one time, a really fun person. We had some good times, but like so many girls in a dying town, it became clear she was looking for a way out, and used not only me, but a lot of other men too.

All three of them quickly scanned the bar. Insecurity at work. Mandy noticed Jameson first and then flitted her eyes over to me. She put a smile on her face, and at her lead, all three girls beelined for us.

"Well guys, that's my cue." I set my empty beer and a twenty dollar bill on the bar for Annie, and I nodded to her for a refill.

"I got it." Jameson nodded at me as I walked toward the head.

I took care of business and by the time I got back to the boys, Mandy and her friends were crowding a foursome of poor unsuspecting men on the opposite side of the room. I knew they were all broke, looking for free booze, and willing to bend over for it.

"How'd you send them off?" I asked as I glanced across the room and leaned over to Jameson.

Jameson was talking to a couple of young pretty girls, being charming as usual, and didn't so much as look my way. That boy could smile the underwear off a nun. Michael leaned back in his corner spot, taking in the entire scene, as usual, not saying a word. Steve leaned over to me and said, "Your brother, very loudly, asked Mandy if she got her test results back and if the sores had gone away yet."

I nearly choked on the beer I just swigged from.

Steve, now chuckling, continued. "They got pissed and walked off. Went and clung to that group of suckers like barnacles," he said, pointing his beer at the group of men that didn't seem to mind all of the feminine attention one bit.

I smiled thinking of my crazy ass brother who didn't care what the hell came out of his mouth and gave him another hearty slap on the back.

I spent the rest of the evening playing a few rounds of pool with my brother. The workload we took in today started to pile up in my mind, and I wanted to get a head start in the morning, so I cut out early leaving Jameson flirting with another set of girls. Steve was nursing a beer at the bar talking to Annie, and Michael? Well, who the fuck knew where Michael went.

The next morning, I was parking a car I had just finished a brake job on, when I saw a girl pedaling a bicycle right into the lot. I recognized the yellow trucker cap, and the pack strapped to her back. She saw me right away, steered her bike toward me and hopped off without coming to a full stop.

"Jesse?"

"Hi, Rina." I knew she'd be coming by, but to suddenly see her again? Damn, she was cute. I clammed up like a teenage boy.

"Do you work here?" she asked, looking around the lot.

"I do. It's my garage. As a matter of fact, I picked up your car for you yesterday. I'm really sorry it's a total loss."

"Yeah, I spoke to somebody named Jameson. He filled me in. He was pretty descriptive with the state of my car." She was brusque and short with her words. Almost like she wanted to run out of there.

I chuckled. "Jameson's my little brother. He's here for the summer until school starts back up. Let's just say, he's sensitive to things with an odor. Do you want to see the car? Get any belongings?"

She nodded, and I led her toward her vehicle. She visibly relaxed and matched my stride. "I can't believe this is your place. What are the chances that of the two people I met this past week, I ran into you twice? Wait. Is your last name Singer?" She stopped abruptly and turned to me.

"Um, yeah. Why?" I knew where this was going.

"Jesse Singer, from Song, PA." This was not a question, and she had a smirk on her face.

"Believe me, the irony is not lost on me. Complete coincidence," I said, smiling back. I heard this pun about my name about a million times over the years. "My brother says you're new to town," I said, changing subjects and trying to keep a friendly discussion going between us.

"Yeah, I lived here years ago when I was a kid, but my grandfather passed on recently, and he left me his house. I was ready for a change, so I packed up and moved in. The house needs a lot of work, but I love it here." She still wasn't looking at me and kept her eyes focused on our destination, but she was smiling when she talked about her house.

"It is a great town," I said. "I've lived in the area all my life." I looked over at her. "You'll like it here."

She didn't respond, as we were now standing in front of her old Corolla. She took a deep breath and dug a set of keys from her pocket and unlocked the trunk. She opened it and stuck her head in.

"I have a few things in the back here—holy shit!" She jumped back, arm stretched across her face. "That's putrid! Oh my God!" She stepped further back from the trunk. She looked at me in terror, her nose scrunched up. I'd say it wasn't the most attractive face, but on her, it looked adorable.

"Yeah, I'm really sorry about that." I cringed. We both took a step back. "I don't know how long that bear was trapped, but from the smell, I'm guessing a good while. With all the stress and panic it suffered, I can't imagine. Add time and heat, and the car was just soaking it all up."

"The poor thing. I hope it's okay." She looked over, walked to the window, then back at me and paled. "Is that blood? Please don't tell me that's blood."

"It could be," I leaned in toward the window. "I feel bad for the bear too. But hey, it seemed okay when it walked into the woods, right? I bet it's fine." We looked at each other. I couldn't read what she was thinking. As soon as I had that thought, she quickly turned away.

Rina looked much like the last time I saw her, tired, unkempt and quite literally, as they say, a hot mess. I supposed she just biked at least five miles to get here. I notices she was obviously fit, looking from her tank top, her shapely breasts, and toned arms.

"Um, I'll just leave what I had in the trunk to the junkyard. It's not worth it." She turned to leave.

I tried to be a gentleman, but I couldn't help staring at her fine ass as she walked ahead of me back toward the bicycle. *Damn.* I fought the urge to adjust myself.

"A bike, huh?" I asked, nodding at the bright green beach cruiser, complete with rear rack and a brown wicker basket.

She tucked a stray hair behind her ear. "Um, yeah. I don't have a vehicle anymore, as you know." She made a sweeping motion toward her car. "I had to find some way to get here. I found a bike at the Thrifty Lot. The man that runs that place is a jerk. I paid more than it was worth, but I was pretty desperate."

I chuffed, "Oh, yeah. Henry Chidders is a cheapskate. He'd charge you for a drink of water, and then a deposit for the cup." I smiled at her. I couldn't help it.

"I believe that," she said with a near smile. "Well, it's done. I have a ride. So, I'm good. I'll have to save up for another car, so that'll be awhile." She looked up at me then and shielded her eyes from the sun so she could look at me. "So what kind of papers do I have to sign?"

"Right. Follow me," I said, and we headed toward the office. On the way there I mulled over Rina's situation. If it were Mandy, or any of the other women I dated in the last few years, it would've never entered her mind to ride a bike or even attempt to solve the problem herself. It would become my problem to fix, and like the sucker I was, I would do it. I admired Rina for finding a way here and then taking steps to fix her situation.

We took care of the paperwork, and I was walking her back through the lot when Jameson pulled in with the tow truck.

"Hey there, Brother, is this the bear girl?" he said leaning out the window of the truck, smirking at Rina.

"Yep, I'm Rina. The bear girl," she said, taking a step toward him. "You must be Jameson." She held out a hand and Jameson grabbed it. "Thanks for the call yesterday. As you can see, I made it here," she said motioning around the lot. She spoke to him with an ease she did not have around me.

"Sorry 'bout the car. I see you're in good hands with Jesse. I've got to pull this into the lot over there. See ya around Rina."

"See you around Jameson," she said, and she watched him pull away.

That little exchange really irritated me. I felt possessive and angry and pissed off at my little brother. What the heck? I didn't know why I was jealous, but I was.

I quelled my anger and instead focused on being friendly. "Let me give you a ride home?" I asked. "I know you have this fine vehicle here, but I'd feel better giving you a ride than making you trek five miles back on your bike, as nice as it is." I silently willed her to say yes.

She frowned deeply and stared at her feet for a minute. Blowing out a deep breath, she looked straight up at me, and said, "You know what? Yes, I'd really appreciate a ride home. Biking around town is one thing, but this was a lot for my first day pedaling a bike since I was twelve years old."

"Ok, give me a minute to clean up and we'll get going."

I left her in the lot while I went to wash off my hands and grab my keys, all the while trying to stay relaxed and calm. I don't know why, but I was nervous. As cleaned up as I could get without getting in a shower, I found Rina strolling the lot looking at all the work I had to get done. We put her bike in the back, and both crawled in the cab of my truck.

"This looks familiar," she said with a grin as she settled herself in, placing her pack on the floor.

"I guess it does. Am I taking you to The Diner, or are you ready to let me take you all the way?"

She looked at me wide eyed for a minute and then her cheeks darkened.

"Home," I amended quickly. "Are you going to show me where you live?"

"You can take me to the house. I guess you're a safe

enough, legitimate guy. Plus, my name and address is on your paperwork. If you were an axe murderer, you'd know where to find me."

"I assure you, Ms. Sullivan, I am not that." I grinned at her as I turned back out of my parking spot and onto the road.

10

Rina

What are the chances that the garage I call is owned by my rescuer from the other night? The hot six foot plus of muscle and hardworking American male I've thought about a dozen times since he left me in that parking lot in the dark. To say he had cleaned up was an understatement. He still had hair a little too long, dark brown and curling around the ears, but his previously unruly beard was now close cut and neatly trimmed. I assumed my memories of him were largely imagined, but is hard muscular and capable body, his blue eyes and genuine smile were right there infant of me. It had to be the haze from an exhausting day and traumatizing event. My mind had to have built that fantasy up. Right? Wrong. I was so wrong it wasn't funny. My imagination had not done him any justice. I felt things low in my belly the second I saw him. Nothing even remotely came close to the desire I instantly felt when he looked at me. I tried desperately to hide it, embarrassed for myself.

He was wearing a navy blue coverall, except he had the top half folded down at the waist. His tight white T-shirt hugged a wide chest that had muscle made from long hours of labor rather than the gym.

I was nervous. My brain was at war with my body all the way home. I should not be having these thoughts. *At all.* I needed to stand on my own two feet. I needed to prove to myself that I was the woman I thought I was. There was also that continuous doubt that the idea he would be attracted to me was preposterous. This guy could get any woman in the world if he wanted, and I was pretty plain. I caught a reflection of myself in the side mirror and was horrified at how tired and haggard I looked. I immediately was embarrassed for myself, again, for even having lustful thoughts.

Yet as my brain flashed warnings all over, my body was melting inside. I could feel my nipples tighten when he lifted my bike into the truck, and I got a good view of his broad back and strong arms at work. I wished he didn't have his coverall folded over his waist, as I'm fairly certain his rear end would not disappoint, if memory served. I was grateful for the slightly padded T-shirt bra I was wearing. And when we were driving down the road, my eyes kept flitting over to his forearm while he shifted gears. Lord have mercy, I felt my underwear dampen.

There was seriously something wrong with me. I was going to hell for all my dirty thoughts. I was so nervous, I couldn't speak. Seriously, I was unable to speak. Jesse tried to make small talk a couple times, and I couldn't manage more than one-word answers until we got close to the house and something in me loosened up and I gained the use of my tongue back.

We pulled onto my street, and panic started in. I wasn't ready to be released from his presence. Now that my voice was working, I wanted to talk.

"Have you had lunch yet? Let me make you lunch. It's the least I could do for you giving me a ride home. And of course, the entire bear incident. I owe you for that."

"That's nice to offer Rina, but I've got to head back. I have lunch plans today. Maybe next time?" He got out of the truck, lifted out my bike, and walked it up toward the porch.

"You're right, this will be a nice house when you get it all cleaned up. Nice street, good location," he said, giving a nosey look around.

I was still stuck on the lunch rejection. "Oh, right, sure thing," I said, trying not to sound defeated. "Well, thank you very much for...well, everything." I was gripping the straps on my backpack, trying not to look fidgety.

"I hope to see you around Rina." He flashed me a killer smile, dropped it as soon as he looked in the rearview to reverse, and pulled out of the drive like he couldn't get out of there fast enough.

I got myself inside, leaned against my shut front door and sighed deeply. *Shit.* Of course, he had a lunch date. Probably a girlfriend. The impossibility of a man like *that* not having a girlfriend was, well, impossible. It was only a sandwich. I wasn't asking for a date for goodness sake. Was I? I reminded myself that I didn't want to be a girlfriend or a date. Actually, I think I muttered that to myself aloud. *Oh God.* This was so embarrassing.

Tomorrow was my first day working at Betsy's Coffee Shop. I knew the pay wouldn't be great, and I'd probably have to find a second, or a better-paying position at some point. But I was grateful for it *and* I had a good feeling about it. Not to mention I liked the idea of having something to do other than going through Grandpa's things, dredging up memories.

It made me sad he spent these last years here alone. I met a couple of the neighbors, but they said he kept to himself, mostly. Puttered around his house and the shed out back. He was neither pleasant, nor unpleasant. I wished he knew that I always missed him, and my memories with him were the only good ones I had in my entire lonely and pathetic life.

"I'm sorry I wasn't there, Grandpa. I'm sorry I wasn't there for a long time." Not for the first time, or the hundredth, I cursed my own mother for her selfishness and lies.

I was not going to let my past get me down. My mother abandoned me long ago and Brad was out of the picture. I would not allow them to hold any influence over my life ever again. I took a deep breath and looked around at the house, the work that needed to be done, and smiled. *Operation: Rina's New Life* begins tomorrow.

11

Rina

"I need a double shot espresso soy latte." Kathy McGearey, the middle aged local real estate agent, called out to me as she trudged through the doors and up to the counter. Working in a coffee shop, I've wondered a thousand times how often customers use the word "need" instead of "want." Caffeine addiction was real and rampant, and it kept little coffee shops all over the world in business.

"You got it, Kath. Coming right up," I said as I cashed her out and started on her coffee. I handed a steaming cup over to her, and Kathy gripped the warm cup two handed.

"Thank you, sweetie, you're a lifesaver."

I smiled back at her.

"And you're my absolute hero, Betsy, for opening up this place. I tell all my clients what a great town we have, and always point out the coffee shop," Kathy said toward Betsy.

"No town is complete without its local java joint, Kath," Betsy hollered over as she wiped down some recently vacated tables.

For the past month, a steady stream of customers filtered in and out of the shop all day, some local, some passing through. This little shop was the stop to make in town. While the rest of Main Street was run down and reminiscent of glory days gone by, once prosperous from the days of the Pennsylvania mining and logging industry, this little place shone like a beacon. It's black- and-white striped awning, charming wrought-iron patio furniture outside, and fifties style decor was inviting to townsfolk and visitors alike. The place was single handedly reviving the shopping strip.

I loved my job, and I loved my new boss. Betsy was like the cool older sister I never had but always wanted.

Turns out the shop had only opened a year ago. After her divorce, Betsy got a good sized settlement from her ex-husband who not only was a serial cheater but had a substantial income. Betsy left the city life behind and opened Betsy's Coffee Shop. She said she wanted to get away from the suits and fancy dinners, the fake faces, and the flashing wealth.

I hadn't told her much about me, but I related. I never wanted to fake myself again. I liked my jeans, T-shirts, and boots. I loved not putting on makeup and simply throwing my hair in a ponytail. I didn't want to impress anybody and certainly didn't want to draw any attention to myself. I just wanted to be me. Most of all, I loved to make people smile when I handed them their cup of coffee in the morning. They weren't judging me by my jeans and T-shirts. It was me and my coffee making skills, and as far as our regular customers were concerned, Betsy and I were the town heroes. Every single morning.

My life had eased into a comfortable routine these past four weeks. I was still pedaling my beach cruiser around. I simply hadn't needed to get a vehicle yet, but I knew I had about eight weeks before fall and then winter arrived. I would have to come up with something. But for now, life was working for me. I worked days at the shop and spent evenings and my days off in my little house.

Betsy gave me good hours, and paid me decently, but she couldn't really do any more. We were barely turning a profit as it was, and I had a feeling she was still paying for a lot of expenses out of pocket. I scraped by on my small salary, mostly because I didn't really have any bills. My house was paid free and clear. I only had utilities and food to cover. Still, there were repairs that needed to be taken care of, and I would have to fund them eventually.

I had a prepaid phone, and nobody to call. It's not like Brad couldn't find me if he wanted to, but I doubted he'd try. He would never stoop so low as to track me down. I made it very clear, before he beat me, that he would never see me again. I only hope that I showed him enough defiance that he wasn't willing to put in the effort to get control over me again. His was a subtle control, and I think he realized he lost that with me, and even if he did get me to stay, the fight would be too great and not worth his effort. He'd just as soon find another to manipulate and control.

Late that afternoon, June, a local hairdresser a few doors down at the Cut 'n Curl, popped in to visit and I mixed up her favorite white chocolate espresso over ice. I liked June. She and Betsy had become instant friends when Betsy moved to town and were of a similar age in their mid-thirties. Where Betsy was loud and bold with her forties movie star looks, June was an understated soccer mom. Her blonde hair was in a simple shoulder-length bob, and she always wore neutral colors and soft fabrics outside of her black hairdresser apron. The two went out regularly for a few drinks and fun, and this would be the third of such outings in the past month. June Ortega was married with two school-aged boys. She rented a booth at the Cut 'n Curl, and she made her own hours around her family. She was always busy and on the go. Her husband, Lou Ortega, was local law enforcement, and liked to come in the shop each morning, always joking with us for not having donuts for him. High school sweethearts, they were both good people.

"Hey there, Junie!" Betsy called out. "Are you ready for some fun tonight?"

"I sure am! Lou is staying home with the boys again. I swear, I am the luckiest woman alive," June said as she plopped down at an empty table.

"Thank you!" She beamed when I handed over her favorite drink. "Hey Rina, you gonna take us up on the offer to join us this time?" June said, a hopeful look on her face.

"I don't know, I'm not a big partier." Crowds weren't really my thing, and the thought of a bunch of drunk men in a loud bar, well...I wasn't sure.

"Aw, come on, Rina. You have to get out and live a little. It'll be fun. There's a band playing over at O'Dells. They're pretty good, and the crowd is usually chill. Lou is going to drop us off, and we'll call him for a ride home." June looked over at Betsy and said again, "Best husband ever."

Betsy nodded in agreement, then turned to me with big

brown pleading eyes. She looked so sincere and was really trying hard to get me to socialize more.

"Ok, I'll go," I said with a genuine smile. I'd been hearing about the local bar, O'Dell's, for a couple weeks now, and June was right, I needed to live a little.

Betsy squealed and came over for a high five. "Yes!"

I don't know how confident I felt when Betsy picked me up later that night, nerves getting the better of me, but I was determined to have myself a good time.

The bar wasn't far. It sat alone on the outskirts of town a few miles from my home. Nestled off a winding tree-lined road, a short drive opened up to a spacious lot. It was the pinnacle of what you'd imagine a roadhouse to be. There were a few motorcycles parked out front, along with an assortment of pickup trucks and the occasional sports car and SUV.

Low and dark, not much adorning the outside, and a long porch with a railing extended down the length of the building. Inside was darker and more run down than I expected, and the crowd was solidly working class. I noticed some younger college types enjoying a drink as well, probably visiting the lakes nearby. This wasn't the uppity crowd of the city with their craft beers and martinis. This was domestic beer and Jack Daniels. The clientele was dressed heavy in denim, and a fair amount of leather. The girls, well they weren't dressed much at all.

We found a small table to the right of the bar. June headed straight to the bartender, a tall pretty blonde that reminded me of a life sized, but kick ass Tinkerbell, and came back with a pitcher of beer and three glasses.

The band was surprisingly good, and I enjoyed the covers of some classic rock favorites. The loud music kept speaking and socializing to a minimum, which I didn't mind at all. Both Betsy and June spent much of their time on the dance floor and didn't give me a hard time when I refused to join them. I kept myself safely between my table and the wall, perfectly happy to be the delegated purse holder and jacket watcher, while I people watched safely tucked away in my corner. I was drinking more than I should, but crowds made me nervous, and the alcohol was helping with that.

Forty-five minutes into the set, June and Betsy were at the table catching a breath from dancing. The door opened to three tall figures. The first I noticed was Jameson, from Singer's Garage, the handsome reddish brown-haired young man with the charming smile. Two more men followed, both as large and as handsome. One had dark hair, skin, and eyes, Italian or Hispanic descent, I guessed. The other was as fair as his friend was dark, with dark blonde hair cropped short on the sides, a trim beard, and looked like he walked off the set of *Vikings*. All three of them over six feet tall, and all three of them too hot for a place like this. All three just, wow. How the heck could such beautiful men be in the same place, let alone together? The crowd in the bar simultaneously parted and leaned toward them as they walked toward the bar in a single line, as if the entire room shared the same unconscious thought. The music was still just as loud, the crowd just as pumped up, but the entire room seemed to take a collective breath, as Jesse, hot guy number four walked in. Now there were four. I felt my panties go instantly damp.

"Damn," Betsy said. "How is it possible that many fine men could walk into the bar at once?"

"That's what I was thinking," I said, never taking my eyes off them.

"I think they're vampires." June propped an elbow on the tall bar table, placing her cheek in her palm. She sighed, captivated.

"Vampires? Where the hell did you get vampires? Those are the Singer's Garage boys," Betsy said in an incredulous voice and rotating her torso as the group of men walked past us and toward the bar. She picked up her beer and took a long drink.

"I know who they are Bets. Doesn't mean they can't be *more* than that. Television and movies. They move in packs just like that. They are beautiful and have a magnetic force that pulls mortals toward them. Enthralled. That's the word. You can't look away," June said as if this were a cold hard fact. "I want one of them to bite me," she said letting out a long breath.

"You're crazy." Betsy laughed and smacked her playfully on the arm. But she followed the men all the way through the bar, like every other victim... um, woman in the place, including myself.

I giggled at my friends bantering back and forth, knowing they were trying to be funny, but June had a point. I couldn't take my eyes off them either, especially Jesse. He walked with purpose to get to the bar, and when he arrived, a beer was waiting. He was wearing a black T-shirt with jeans and work boots. His hair was just the right amount of messy, but unlike men who made an effort, he obviously did not. He just had perfect hair that was naturally sexy. Everything about the guy oozed sex. Who was I kidding? He grabbed his beer and turned around, elbows propped back onto the bar top to watch the band. I couldn't stop staring. And, as if he knew he was being eye stalked, he scanned the crowd and locked eyes on me.

He smiled genuinely and lifted his beer to me. I did the same back with my cup and cracked an embarrassed smile. Caught looking, *shit*. I could feel Betsy and June collectively turn their heads and gawk at me—June's mouth slightly agape, and Betsy cracking a smile. I said nothing. A crowd of scantily clad women descended upon the four men, and the magic was lost. The room felt like it started to move again. I lost sight of them all.

"What was that?" Betsy asked.

"What?" I asked.

"I saw it too!" June piped in, pointing a finger at me.

"Nothing. That's the guy that rescued me from the bear." I shrugged. "He's nice."

"He's *nice*?" This from Betsy, lifting one eyebrow. I was always jealous of people that could do that.

"Look, it's nothing. I think he has a girlfriend, okay? It's nothing."

They must've sensed my wanting to drop it and they did, like good friends should. Betsy grabbed June's hand and pulled her out to the dance floor, but not without a wink and a, "We'll talk about this later," smirk on her face.

"Hey there," a not-so-bad looking man, clean cut and with a friendly smile said to me.

I was alone at the table debating whether to call a cab and go home. I wasn't bored, exactly. I had a nice time, but the noise was starting to get to me. I much preferred quiet things like hiking, sitting on my porch, or watching movies.

"Hello." I stayed on my side of the table. I gave a courteous smile, but nothing more. Please somebody rescue me. I tried not to be too obvious looking for Betsy or June, but I really wasn't here to get hit on.

"Come dance with me? You look so lonely over here," the guy said.

It felt too forced, and that clean cut exterior hid something I didn't like. Polite works more often than you'd think, so I went for that.

"No thanks. I'm good." I started looking around for my friends, trying to look disinterested and get the guy to leave.

He didn't get the hint. "Buy you a drink? You look like you need a drink."

I raised my half cup of beer and stared at him deadpan. Time to shut this down. "Look, I'm a polite girl, so I'm going to be real nice here. I'm not interested. Not in you, not in anybody. I'm having a fun night out with my girlfriends and I'd like to keep it that way."

"Okay, okay. I get it. I know when to walk away."

He smiled at me, and though his words and mannerisms weren't threatening, something about that smile raised the hairs on the back of my neck. But he backed off and disappeared into the dancing crowd. I looked around the bar for the girls and caught them laughing and wiggling out on the floor. I smiled at them having fun.

I scanned some more and caught eyes with Jesse for the second time that night. A tall blonde had an arm around his shoulder and crawled up on his lap. His girlfriend. She was beautiful, but I was surprised to note, a little trashy. Huh. I wasn't expecting that from a guy like Jesse. She had long, blonde, straight hair that fell over her shoulders. Her makeup was expertly applied, eyes lined in a way I would never be able to copy no matter how many YouTube videos I watched. From her eyebrows to her lips, she was flawless. Let's not talk about her body. She had a deep navy-blue dress on that left nothing to the imagination. She filled every corner of that dress like a second skin.

I felt a pang of jealousy. I could never come close to that. I had tried, of course. Brad always wanted my hair and makeup perfect. I was to wear fashionable and well fitted professional attire every time we went out together. God forbid I wore a pair of jeans. I snorted at myself. If he could see me now. Tight jeans, fitted T-shirt and cowboy boots. I left my hair down tonight, but also wore no makeup except for some mascara and tinted lip balm.

At heart, I'm not a dress up kind of girl, and if I wanted to be true to myself, I had to let all of my inadequacies go. I had to accept that as sexy as Jesse was, if that was the type of girl he wanted, I was not that, and I would never be that. Most importantly, I was not going to change anything about me ever again for a man. Despite my internal girl power pep talk, I really wanted to be on his lap, damnit. I squirmed my way out of the safety of my corner and headed to the ladies' room.

12
―――

Jesse

I really didn't want to go to O'Dell's tonight, but the guys talked me into it. A local band was playing, and I did like their music. So after I finished up my last job, I cleaned up and headed over. It was a late night at the garage. I usually like to close up by 6:00, but I needed to get this latest restoration started to hopefully make some extra cash.

With bills and a heavy workload on my mind, I was already irritated trying to move through the crowd at the bar. Thank goodness Annie had a beer waiting when I made it to the guys. That girl always had a beer waiting for me, and I appreciated it. I think there was something between her and Steve. I wasn't sure what, but there was an obvious tension between the two of them.

My mood instantly lifted when I saw Rina at a table at the other end of the bar. She had stuffed herself in the far corner, keeping the table between herself and the crowd. Back against the wall, view of the entire floor. Smart girl. I didn't imagine I'd see her here, but it was a small town, I knew I'd run into her sooner or later. I lifted my beer to her and smiled. She smiled back and looked off to the band. I recognized the two women with her. Betsy ran the new coffee shop, and was relatively new to town, and Lou Ortega's wife. She worked at the Cut 'n Curl, and had a couple kids. Both women were a few years older than me, and probably a decade older than Rina. Nonetheless, they seemed like they were close to Rina, and I liked that she found some people. Rina glanced over at me again before resuming her conversation.

I drank another couple beers, listened to a couple songs, and had more than a couple of women trying to cram into our bar space. One of which was Mandy, who couldn't get the picture and tried to actually crawl into my lap. I always try to be nice to women. I used to not be picky. Pussy was pussy, right? Since I was sixteen, I've had a string of nameless women crawling in and out of my bed. Every once in a while I tried to create a relationship. I tried with Mandy, even though I knew she wasn't my type. Call me an asshole, but I stayed with her because it was easier to just give her the things she wanted than listen to her whine and complain. She started talking about me buying her a house and giving her a car, and I realized I had let it go on too long. And then she fucked me over. The unforgivable kind, and after that I vowed to never get myself in that position again. When she crawled into my lap at the bar, I was firm.

"Mandy, I told you, not for the first time, we are over." I put my hands around her waist to nudge her to get off me.

Instead, she wrapped an arm around my neck and leaned

in. "Come on, baby, I miss you. Let's go out back. My mouth wants your cock."

I could smell the alcohol on her breath.

"I think you'll need to find someone else for that," I said as I lifted her off me and stood.

"You're an asshole, Jesse Singer," she hissed.

There it is, I thought. That pretty face gone. Replaced by a vicious, ugly snarl in an instant.

I stood and started to back away. "Look, just leave okay?" I said.

"Fucker," she spat and strode off.

Mandy wasn't always so hate filled and angry. She used to be pretty sweet and kind. We'd enjoyed each other's company for a long time, but since things between us went south, she kept descending. Instead of moving on, she went out. As is out every night and drinking excessively. She started wearing too much makeup and dressed in too tight clothes, as if she was telling the world not to look too close. I didn't know what was going on with her.

I headed over toward the restroom just to get out of there. I squeezed my way through the now liquored-up crowd and strode down the long dark corridor. It wasn't unusual to find folks back there getting it on, and I saw a familiar silhouette of two entangled bodies toward the end. I was just about to push open the door, when I heard a muffled, "Get off me." I turned my head and realized that the feminine figure was pushed hard against the wall and was struggling.

"Hey!" I growled as I walked toward them.

The man extended one hand toward me, head down, his face close to the girl. "We're good here, man, go away."

"Get. Off. Of. Me." I heard the girl again, and I could see her struggling under the larger man's weight.

I went red inside, realizing it was Rina. I hardly knew the woman, but I knew there was no way she'd willingly be in this hallway with a douche like this guy. I grabbed the guy by the shoulder and pulled him off.

"What the fuck?" The guy spun around, fist raised. He stopped mid motion when he not only took in my size, but I'm sure he could see the fury written all over my face.

"Go," I stormed. "Get out of here before you regret it." The asshole took off without a word.

I looked down at the girl, who was using the wall to straighten herself up.

"Shit, Rina. Are you okay?" I asked, reaching toward her.

She folded in on herself and put her hands out. "I'm okay."

I leaned in and she shrunk back. I lifted my hands and stepped back, giving her space.

"I'm alright, honest." She looked down the hallway where the guy left. "That asshole. He was badgering me earlier and caught up with me coming out of the restroom." I could see her hands shaking as she straightened her shirt and ran her hands through her hair. She took a deep breath and looked around the now quiet hallway again. "I guess I have to thank you for saving me once again, Jesse Singer."

She took another deep breath and looked up at the ceiling. I could see her trying not to cry. I just stood there, waiting for her to collect herself. "I didn't even want to come out here tonight, you know. Crowds aren't really my thing. Of course, something like this happens and ruins the good time I was managing to have."

"You can still have a good time. I'll show you a good time." She looked quickly at me and blushed furiously.

"Oh... no, sorry. I didn't mean it like that. Honest. I just meant come over and sit with me and my guys. We'll look after you."

"I'm, um, no thanks. My luck I'd get jumped again, this time by a horde of skanky bar flies. Plus, I don't think your girlfriend would appreciate that."

"My girlfriend?" I questioned.

"Yeah, that pretty blonde sitting on your lap earlier."

"Oh Jesus, Mandy? That girl is not my girlfriend. Well, she used to be, but it's a really long terrible story. I broke it off half a year ago. She's having a hard time understanding me. I may have to sign her up for an English class or something," I joked.

"Oh, sorry. I didn't know. I think I'm done here. Betsy and June are having such a great time. I think I'm just gonna call a cab and go home."

"No," I said, too quickly. Being this close to her again, I realized that I did not want to let her leave.

"No?" she asked.

"You are not calling a cab. I'll take you home."

"I cannot let you ruin your night! I'm fine, really," she protested.

"Look, it's not even up for discussion. It'll take forty-five minutes for a cab to get here anyway."

"Are you sure?"

"I'm more than sure. I wasn't in the mood to go out tonight either. I've had a long day, and I just want to sit in front of my TV and watch the Friday night TCM classic, with me, myself and a beer."

She quirked her head at me. "Did you say classic film? I love classic films. What's your favorite? I love everything from Greta Garbo to eighties John Hughes films."

I stared at her, stunned. Her smile and the way her eyes just lit up had my tongue tied for a moment. I shook myself out of it. "They are having a triple header tonight on AMC, I think the late night was *Sunset Boulevard* with—"

"William Holden! Oh, I love that one. Damn, I wish I had cable."

"I do," I said.

She looked at me, eyes wide.

"Want to come to my place and watch a movie?" At her skeptical look, I added, "This is not a pick up. Honest. I'm just excited to have somebody over to talk movies with. Have you seen the people in this place? Imagine talking *Dead End Kids* with these folks. I'm serious. Just a friendly movie night with two people that dislike crowds."

"Oh, *Dead End Kids* is always so overlooked! One of Bogart's best if you ask me. Yes, actually, I think I would really like that."

13

Rina

Here I was, once again climbing into Jesse Singer's truck.

"Hello, my old friend," I said to her and patted the dash. Jesse climbed in the other side. While he pulled out of the lot, I texted Betsy and told her I found a ride home with a friend. I told her I was fine, and to have a good time. I thanked her for taking me out.

It wasn't a bad night, aside from the asshole in the hallway pushing me up against the wall trying to kiss me. Jesse arrived at the moment I realized I was not able to push him off and was about to kick the guy in the balls and start screaming, loudly.

But it was looking like my evening was going to get better. I did still want to crawl into Jesse Singer's lap, but the idea of hanging out with a "friend" was appealing too. I was more relaxed around Jesse. Maybe because the man had come to my rescue more than once now, and I could genuinely see he was a nice guy. Maybe it was because I had a few drinks. Or maybe it was because I knew what type of women he went for, and I so clearly was not it—I didn't mind being friend-zoned. It took a lot of pressure off. Friends? I can do that.

Jesse pulled into the Singer's Garage parking lot.

"You live here?" I asked.

"Yup, I have an apartment above the shop. I'd like to buy a house, but I have some things to settle up before I can do that," he said as we pulled around back.

A set of wooden steps led up the side of the large building. We walked up and he led me inside. The apartment was bigger than I thought it would be. It was loft-like with a large living, kitchen, dining area. There was a small hallway off toward the back that looked like it led to a couple bedrooms and a bath. In the middle of the room stretched an L shaped sectional sofa in front of a large flat screen TV mounted on the wall. The furniture was brown. The walls were white and bare, except for a calendar of a pinup girl near the door. The place screamed bachelor pad. There were a few auto magazines scattered on the coffee table, and a few pictures of Jesse, Jameson, and an attractive older woman on a small sideboard table near the entrance.

Jesse grabbed the remote off the coffee table and turned on the TV.

"Have a seat; make yourself at home." He went off into the kitchen area, while I took off my shoes and sat in the middle of the sofa. It was a big sofa. I agonized for a sec where I should sit and then said screw it, sat in the best spot, and curled up like it was my own. Jesse came back from the kitchen with a couple cans of soda and a large bowl of popcorn.

"Popcorn? Who just has popcorn in their cupboard ready to go?" I laughed.

"Me. Always. No movie is complete without popcorn. Popcorn is life in this house. You can buy it in big bags. It's the perfect snack food."

I took the proffered soda, and Jesse sat down next to me, as dead center as he could get, putting the bowl between us.

"Looks like we're early enough to catch the second half of *Some Like it Hot*," he said with a grin. "I love the dance numbers."

Ok, this guy was insanely gorgeous, more than nice, and well, kind of a geek.

"Are you gay?" I barely had the thought before it came bursting out of my mouth. "Oh my God, I'm so sorry. I don't even know why I asked that. It's none of my business. And I don't care, or rather, I don't really think that's true. Of course, you're not gay. Oh my God, I'm so embarrassed."

"What? No!" His reaction was so comical. He looked guilty. "I mean, gay people are cool. It's just not who I am." We were both silent in the awkward moment. Finally, Jesse cleared his throat and said, "My mom loves these old movies, and when I was a kid, we'd watch them together."

He laughed out loud and then turned to me. "I assure you, I am not gay." His eyes roamed my face, and paused at my lips for a long moment, then they traveled to my collarbone and down to my breasts. "I can show you if you like."

His lips were parted, and he glanced up and met my eyes. My heart started racing, my nipples hardened under his stare, and heat started pooling at things down below.

"Stop it!" I forced myself to say with a girly squeal. "You're terrible! Okay, you are NOT gay. And let me just say, it would be a terrible tragedy for women everywhere if that were true. There are enough beautiful men on the other team, thank you very much." I turned red again.

He didn't seem to be bothered by the comment, but laughed and patted my thigh like I was a favorite pet. "Movie?"

"That's right, movie buddies, nice guy." *Beautiful, smoking hot, I just want to crawl in your lap and lick you, nice guy.* I took a deep breath and settled in to watch a movie.

14

Jesse

This girl was hot, and she didn't even know it. After the gay comment, I couldn't resist teasing her. When my eyes traveled down the length of her, my dick definitely caught notice. She blushed furiously; it was adorable. I had no idea what her deal was, but there was definitely something up. I didn't want to spook her, and I did not want to make any sudden moves. I was reasonably confident I could have her in my bed by the end of the evening, but I didn't want that. I wanted a girl that could also be a friend, and this girl looked like she could use one. I didn't want to ruin that by throwing her in my bed like a caveman. Being new here, the only people she knew were her boss and the local hairdresser, which was great, but she definitely wasn't a social butterfly.

We watched the two movies together and talked during

the commercials. I learned a little during those brief intermissions. She was an only child. No parents, but I don't think they were dead. Just not around. She liked her job making coffee, but I had a feeling she needed more than that.

During one commercial break I asked, "So you like hiking? I figured since we met up off Parson's, you like the outdoors."

"I love hiking. I know there must be a lot of great trails around here, but I haven't had much of a chance to explore. Plus, you know, the bear thing kind of freaked me out. I probably should buy some of that bear spray."

"Hiking is one of my favorite things. I don't like crowds much, so I usually like to hike when I have time. I can take you and show you some good spots. And I'll protect you from the bears."

"Really? I would love that. My body could really use the release."

"I can help with that too." I winked at her.

"Stop it!"

She blushed deep crimson again, and it was beautiful. I wanted to make her blush every day.

"You know what I mean, there is nothing like a good hike. It feeds the soul. When is your next day off?"

"Friday, unless Betsy needs me." She answered.

"Friday, we hike," I announced.

It was nearly two a.m. when the credits started rolling, and Rina had fallen asleep on the sofa. She looked so adorable, all curled up into a tight little ball. I didn't have the heart to wake her. I took the blanket off of Jameson's bed and covered her up. I left him a text letting him know I was leaving the bar, but I hadn't heard a word from him. I assumed at this hour, he wouldn't be coming home, and I guaranteed that boy ended up at some girl's house.

I woke at 7:00 a.m. to the sound of laughing from the kitchen. The smell of coffee got me out of bed. I pulled on a pair of sweatpants and walked out to see Rina sitting at the kitchen table, coffee mug cradled in two hands. Jameson was leaning against the counter finishing what sounded like an account of the previous evening.

"And just like out of the movies, I jumped out the window. Thank goodness it was on the first floor. Haven, the girl's name was Haven, started chucking all of my clothes out behind me. I was wondering why she had me park on the street and not pull into the drive. Turns out her boyfriend worked the night shift and was in the driveway."

"You are an asshole," I said as I poured myself a cup. "Good morning, Rina." I nodded over to her.

"Good morning," Rina said. She couldn't hide the fact that she was staring at my shirtless top half, but she made an effort to be nonchalant.

"She didn't tell me, Brother," Jameson broke in. "Honest, I would never have gone home with her had I known! I wish some women would just fix their shit, you know? I have feelings too. I feel used."

"You're only saying that because Rina's here."

Rina didn't even try to hide her grin.

"Yes, Rina—who I found on the sofa this morning. What happened last night?" he said wiggling his eyebrows with a grin.

"We watched movies together," Rina said. "*Sunset Boulevard*."

"No way! My brother found the only other person on the planet that likes AMC? He's such a nerd. One time he took an entire day off to watch the Monster Classic Bash."

"Fuck off. They were playing *Dracula*, *The Mummy*, and then later *American Werewolf in London*."

"I would've done the same thing. *American Werewolf in London* is fantastic. And Boris Karloff." She looked over at me, then back at Jameson. "You call Jesse a nerd, I guess you'll have to call me one too," Rina said, defending me.

A slow grin spread across Jameson's face. He looked back and forth between us. "I *cannot wait* to see how this turns out," and walked off to the shower.

"I'm sorry about him. He's related, so I'm forced to take care of him," I said apologizing.

"I like him. He doesn't hide much, does he?" Rina asked.

"No, he does not. Don't let him fool you though. He's smart as shit. He'll only be here a few more weeks until the next semester starts. Then he's back up at State. His last year. I can't wait until he's out of here taking up space in my apartment." I shook my head in disappointment. "Trying to humiliate me in front of beautiful women, it's exhausting."

"He seems like a good guy, and good for him for finishing school. Your family must be proud," Rina said.

"My mom is. She lives down in Florida now in one of those fifty-five and over communities."

When Rina didn't say anything at all, I continued.

"My dad took off early on. She pretty much raised Jameson and I on her own. She put in twenty years at the plant and retired early after an accident left her with limited use of her right arm. Over time and with a lot of physical therapy, she's seventy-five percent recovered, but that's as good as it's going to get. The plant was fair, she got a decent pension, and she's made a good little life for herself."

"Well, looks like she did good raising you and Jameson," Rina said.

"How about you, you've hardly told me much about you?" I asked, but immediately regretted it as I watched her face close down.

"Not much there. Like I said, It's just me."

She shifted uncomfortably, and I let her. It was a dick move, but I wanted to know more.

Rina continued on. "I lived here as a kid. I have some amazing memories of my grandfather. I like it here. I'm looking to have a future here." She stood up, placing her mug in the sink. "I hate to ask, but I've got to get going. I have a list of things to take care of. Do you think you could give me a ride?"

I had come up with this idea last night and mulled it over some more this morning. "I have this kind of crazy idea, and I don't think you're going to like it, but hear me out."

Her posture straightened, and she crossed her arms.

"It may be better if I show you. Let me throw some clothes on and I'll be right out." I stepped quickly into my room and grabbed a T-shirt. When I came into the living area, Rina was by the door stepping into her boots. She looked up at me warily.

"It's nothing to worry about. Come on," I assured her and opened the door. She followed me down the back steps into the lot. "Stay here." I quickly ducked into the garage and swiped a set of keys off the hanger. When I came back out, I grabbed her hand, immediately loving the feel of it clasped in my own, and said, "Over here." I led her across the lot and stopped in front of the old Chevy.

"This is a 1985 Chevy C-10 pickup. I've had it here in the lot for two years. She's my personal restoration project that I haven't had a moment to work on." Before Rina could protest, I rushed on. "It's not much to look at, and there are a ton of cosmetic issues. But it runs, and the tires are good. I use it occasionally for hauling parts around." I realized I was rambling and stopped.

"No. I can't." Rina was shaking her head.

"Why not? Look, it's just sitting here." I pointed at it. It was true. The truck was barely used, and I didn't have time for her just yet. I thought it was a brilliant idea.

"I can't, this is too much. You want to give me a truck? You hardly know me."

"I'm not giving you a truck," I insisted. "I'm letting you borrow a truck that I don't use. It would actually be good for the engine if it ran every day. You'd be doing me a favor. Insurance is even paid up until the end of the year. But if you want to *borrow* it, and I do mean borrow, I'm offering. No strings attached. I'd honestly be happy if you used it."

"Where did you come from, Jesse Singer?" She looked at me in wonder.

I just smiled. "I've always been here."

15

Rina

I've always been here.
This guy is too much. I stood there, once again, dumbfounded. I didn't know if I should run away or throw myself at him. If I was honest, I wanted to rip off his clothes and impale myself on his cock right here in the parking lot. A truck? The guy rescued me from a bear, rescued me from a sleaze in a bar, and now he was offering me a truck.

"I don't know what to say." I really didn't. Truthfully, I needed this truck badly. I was beginning to stress about the upcoming winter. I was picturing myself walking to work in snow shoes.

"Just say, 'Thanks, Jesse, see you Friday.'"

I walked over and hugged him. Okay, let's be honest here, I threw myself at him and his big, lovely arms folded around me instantly. He was large and warm, and he smelled amazing, a woody spice with the faintest tinge of oil. He smelled like all man, and I swear I started salivating. I felt his strong back and hard muscles through his shirt, and it took all I had not to start groping his body or lick his neck. Holy shit. When his arms wrapped around me, I felt instantly safe and simultaneously like running. It scared the shit out of me. I tried to remember the last time I was hugged by somebody, and I couldn't. I swear, it was the single best and most sensual hug I've ever had in my life.

"Thank you," I whispered next to his ear. He was so close. The stubble of his beard caressed my face. He pulled back, hands gently holding my upper arms. One hand slid to my cheek, and his thumb lazily grazed my jaw. I looked up into his eyes, and a flash of heat blazed before he took a deep breath and stepped back.

"Right. Yes, here are the keys. Take good care of her. I'll see you Friday, Rina."

"See you Friday, Jesse."

The truck wasn't pretty by any stretch of the imagination. It was a dingy white with patches of primer from sporadic and unfinished body work. The interior was even worse. Bare metal ceiling, rips in the seats, and an honest to goodness tennis ball on the manual gear shift. I loved her instantly.

I hoisted myself into the cab and turned the engine over. She bit into a roar. I shifted into reverse and backed out of there.

As I made my way back to the house, I made a mental list of things to do. I also thought about Jesse. A lot. My gut told me that it was just as it seemed. A genuine good guy who had several opportunities to help a girl out and went with it.

However, Brad started out much the same. He gave me everything, or so my nineteen year-old self told me. I didn't realize how much he took away until I got that visit from the lawyer. Reflecting on the past five years, and realizing how badly I was manipulated, tears formed in my eyes. Five years. I lost five years of my life. All I had been was a doll for Brad to hang on his arm. To look coiffed and perfect for his work colleagues. To cook his meals for him. To please him in bed.

I inwardly groaned at those thoughts. I was ashamed. Brad was not an attentive lover. Never once did he consider pleasing me, but he always let me know what he wanted. There were many days he walked in the door and called me to him.

"Katrina!" When I'd arrive at the doorway, he'd smile at me as he started unbuckling his expensive work slacks. "Katrina, I had such a hard day baby, I need you to suck me off." And he'd push his pants down, his not overly generous dick springing free of his briefs. And God help me, I did it. I'd get down on my knees and pleasure him. When I'd finish, Brad would be so approving. Saying things like, "Oh, how I love you. Oh, you are so good to me, baby."

And I would think that he did love me. That I did good. That pleasing him was what I was supposed to do for my man, and this was how I repaid all of the kindnesses for him taking care of me. He told me often enough, that I owed him so much. Sometimes in the morning, when I was brushing my teeth in our en suite bath, Brad would come up behind me, wrap an arm around my waist and take me from behind. When he was finished, he'd leave me breathless, alone and empty, and say, "I'm so happy I have you to take care of my morning erections."

My stomach roiled, and I wanted to vomit. The tears were rolling down my face now as I thought back to those times. Was it consensual? Yes. He never raped me. He never raped me because I never resisted. I never said no. But it was still abuse. I see that now. I was nothing but a whore who allowed herself to be used over and over, for what? I see now that I had nothing. I had no friends, no job, no education. Nothing to show for my life. I didn't know who I was.

Shame engulfed me as I thought of Jesse. I imagined him in my bed, on top of me, caressing me. Something told me that he'd be attentive to a woman's sexual needs. *Screech! Put that thought on hold, Rina.* I was not ready to go there yet. I wanted to find myself. I was apprehensive of sex right now anyway, even with somebody as seemingly nice as Jesse, no matter how badly my body betrayed me when he was around. I was scared of the things it might trigger inside me. I was not a weak girl. I was not going to let Brad take any more of me. I was well on my way to building a new life, and I wasn't going to mess this up. I got a second chance. I was going to keep it.

By the time I arrived home, I was resolved to get more housework done. My new home was old and full of, well, old people stuff. I had slowly been cleaning up, but I really needed to do some serious getting rid of things. I started making piles of boxes in the corner of the living room. A pile for trash, a pile for charity. A pile for memories. It was hard. Going through somebody's entire life and deciding what to do with their things. I had so much guilt for not being there. I'm grateful that Grandpa hadn't gotten sick and had nobody to care for him. I don't think I could've lived with that, knowing that he didn't disown me after all, and it was my mother and her lies that kept us apart. I could barely live with it now. I wasn't ready to get into my mommy issues just yet. That anger was a long time simmering, and I just didn't have the energy to ponder why a mother would abandon her daughter and keep her away from her only other living relative. Grandpa had a heart attack and died on the front lawn. The mail carrier found him that same afternoon.

Practicality won out. So much was of no use and I didn't want it. I don't think Grandpa would've minded me getting rid of the old magazines, clothes and knick-knacks that one accumulates over a lifetime. Drawers full of odds and ends. Too much stuff crammed into every nook and cranny in the place. I couldn't stand it anymore. I read an article once that clutter can cause depression and decluttering could be therapeutic. It was working. I was honestly feeling better with each bit of progress I made. I kept at a good pace, and near the end of the afternoon, my piles were taking shape and threatened to overflow into the dining room, but I called it progress.

I was working my way through the built-in bookshelf in the living room, stuffed full of old *Guns and Ammo* magazines, *Hunter's Digest*, and *Field and Stream*, when I found it. A spiral-bound notebook with the hand written title *Eleanor Rose Hannigan's Baking Secrets*.

Eleanor Rose Hannigan was my grandmother. There were photos of her all over the house. Grandpa had often spoken of her as if she was in the house along with us all. He loved her more than anything. I have memories of him telling me, "Katrina, when you find the love of your life, never let go. No matter what, never let go."

She died long before I was born when my mother was only seventeen. She was driving home from the grocery when she hit black ice and went off the road. It was the town tragedy at the time, and Grandpa said she was so lovely the entire town mourned her loss. My grandfather never looked at another woman. He always said, "I was lucky enough to find the love of my life. Eleanor was it."

Eleanor's baking was legendary when I was a child. Grandpa never stopped talking about her cakes and muffins and cookies. He said she had a "secret ingredient" for everything. He could never eat a single dessert without mentioning it. When I had thoughts of who my grandmother was, I pictured her in this very kitchen, in a pretty floral dress, wearing an apron, and pulling out a pan of muffins from the oven.

I sat on the floor with the book. The notebook was well worn. The pages were falling out from abuse and neglect, and the cardboard backing was about to disintegrate. On each page, written in neat cursive handwriting, was a recipe. I hugged the book to my chest. All this time, Grandpa had kept this treasure. I wonder if he read through the recipes? Why did he never share this with my mother or me when we were here? I would've loved to bake these recipes. And like a light bulb in a comic, an idea suddenly formed in my mind.

While I was headed out, I loaded up the bed of the truck with stuff to drop off at the Goodwill, and I made myself a shopping list.

Eleanor Rose wrote a very specific introduction in her

book about technique and rules of baking to never stray from. There was a very clear message to never break any of her baking rules. The first rule was to "Always wear your apron. It completes your persona." So when I dropped off the donations at the Goodwill, I also found a rose printed apron hanging on the edge of a rack. It felt as if Eleanor was watching me from above and guiding my way.

I spent the rest of the evening in the kitchen, trying to teach myself to bake. I could cook, of course. Those five years of living with Brad and keeping house had ensured it. I could even classify myself as a very good cook, from roasts to pasta. One had to be when Brad insisted on never having the same meal twice each week, and never anything from a can or a freezer. But a baker, I was not.

Brad never wanted to have sweets and cakes in the house, claiming it wasn't good for our figures. Namely, he didn't want me to gain any weight. While I'm certain he indulged at each company lunch and dinner, I was careful to not "let myself go," as he would put it. Even when eating my carefully prepared meals, Brad would often say, "Your portion looks the same as mine, Katrina, and I have a good fifty pounds on you."

I would then return food from my plate. I was not a large woman by any means, but I am not tiny. I'd consider myself average, with enough curves to fit my tailored clothes nicely, but at 5'4" and what one may consider an athletic build, I would never be a model.

Since Grandpa had apparently never let anything go in the house, I found an old mixer in the kitchen and several baking pans. I was certain these were the same that Eleanor used all those years ago.

In that kitchen reading through the recipe book, wearing my rose printed apron, and using the baking pans and mixer, I felt my life changing. Something deep inside told me I was headed in the right direction, and that Eleanor Rose and Jesse Singer were both somehow part of it.

16

Jesse

I'd been slammed busy the last few days and was looking forward to taking off tomorrow to take Rina hiking. I wasn't complaining, I really needed the extra cash the business was bringing in. All of my guys were at the shop today. Even Jameson was helping out with the three tow calls we got this morning. Mundane repairs like breaks, timing belts and fuel pumps were our bread and butter, but restoration was where I could make a big profit on a small investment. Unfortunately, customers' needs came first, and restorations kept getting pushed back.

Each of us were at various stations around the shop. Classic rock was blaring through the big room and we were working steadily. Steve did all of our body work. The man was an artistic genius and was currently working on banging out a few dents on a Camry that got dinged up in a parking lot fender bender. He was singing along rather loudly and off key, but having a great time with himself, a hammer, and a sheet of metal. I'd occasionally catch sight of his short dark hair bobbing in time to the music from the other side of the car.

Michael, one of the most talented mechanics I knew, was running through a slew of diagnostics on a Dodge Ram pickup that was giving its owner all kinds of problems. Quiet as always, Michael stared at the screen, jotting down notes while stroking his blond beard. They were both great guys who'd came to Singer's through happenstance.

When old man McGrady decided to retire to the sunny state of Florida and hang up his tool belt, I bought the garage, and renamed it Singer's. McGrady was a decent guy who earned enough of a living and saved enough for retirement. I had apprenticed at his place since high school, and when he left, he offered to carry the loan. He said I was the only person on the planet he trusted not to run the place in the ground, and not to rip off customers.

Steve answered an ad I had posted for a body mechanic. He's the most talented paint and body guy I've seen, and I'm lucky he's at Singer's to not only work on scratch and dents, but my restoration projects. Steve needed to get out of Texas and away from some business he never talked about, and I never asked. I know he had it really rough growing up, and I have the feeling he was mixed up in some seedy business. All he ever told me was if he stayed in Texas, he would end up behind bars or in the ground. He's been a great employee and friend, and treats the shop and the crew like family.

Michael wandered in one day after he bought a house with some land nearby. Raised by a working class family in

Maine. He went to college and earned himself some sort of engineering degree. While his family wasn't happy that he left the engineering field, I think they eventually accepted his choice for a simpler life of working with his hands. He still did some type of work from his home, which is why he only came in part time, but I wasn't exactly sure what that was.

Jameson, my little brother, is headed into his last year at university in wildlife studies. He's one of the most laid back and happy guys I know. He did qualify for several partial scholarships, but he still had to pay some tuition, and I did my best to help. My mother did her damned best to raise us, and I didn't want to burden her with taking care of Jameson. I want her to take care of herself. She deserves it.

My father left when I was seven, the year Jameson was born. The day she found out she was having another boy, my mom asked my father what they should name him. My dad looked down at the bottle in his hand and said, "Jameson," and walked out the door.

That pretty much explains who my father was right there. He was gone before Jameson's first birthday. Being seven years older, and having made so many mistakes myself, I've done my best to guide him. He doesn't remember those early years of Mom working double shifts six days a week to keep the lights on, and I don't want him to. He is a twenty-one-year-old goofball though, always into a good time, and always in a woman's pants. And as demonstrated earlier this week, sometimes his wandering dick lands him in places it shouldn't. He does appreciate all that I've done to help him out though, so every summer he helps out at the shop when he can.

Jameson had just finished unhooking a broken down

Ford Taurus, when he walked into the shop with Rina on his heels.

"Jesse, look what I found outside," he hollered across the room.

He had to yell pretty loudly on account of the music, but he got my attention. Rina stood there in the entrance, with a large basket looped around her forearm. I turned down the volume on the speaker before walking over to where she was standing. She had her signature jeans and boots on with a tightly fitted T-shirt that read, "I got a Latte Problem." Her light brown hair softly curled around her shoulders, and her eyes crinkled as a smile lit up her face. She was adorable. I wanted her; God help me.

"Hey there, Jesse," She said in greeting. "I tried to send you a text earlier, asking if it was alright if I stopped by, but then I figured I'd just take the chance you were here. Hope that's alright," she said looking up at me, worrying her bottom lip.

"You can stop by anytime," I said. She'd been on my mind all week. I kept replaying that hug over and over again. Her soft body curled into mine. I felt like a thirteen-year-old kid, and all I wanted to do was to hug her again. Of course, other things sprung to mind too. I tried to shut those thoughts down real quick, as soon as my dick started stirring. If the guys saw me with a hard on at work, they would never let it go.

"Hey guys, this is Rina, the girl whose car the bear ate," I announced to the room.

"I guess I will forever be known as..." Rina said, smiling, a pink blush spread across her cheeks.

"Hey there, Rina, I'm Steve," Steve said walking over and scoping her out the closer he got.

I wanted to growl at him. Steve was easily the biggest flirt in my life. The guy made my *mother* blush when she visited last summer. He reached out and shook her hand.

"We all know about your car. That was the funniest thing and the saddest thing I've ever seen happen to a car. And I've seen a lot. It was worth it though to see Jameson lose his lunch."

"Fuck off, man. I'm sensitive, you know," Jameson whined.

"So yeah, this is Steve, and that over there is Michael." Michael stayed where he was, and tilted his chin up in a hello. That was as much as anybody got from him until he got to know them. As far as I know, Michael only talked to us, and whatever he did at his other job at home. The man got more pussy than Jameson, I swear. I don't think I've ever seen him actually have a conversation with a woman, but I sure have seen him exiting the back seat of a few cars, or buttoning up his jeans turning a corner around the outside of O'Dell's. Women went crazy over the silent Viking thing he had going on.

Rina waved a little finger hello to Michael, and I swear she blushed at him. He didn't offer her more than the slightest smile. Fucker. What was it with my guys making Rina blush a lot?

"Um, anyway, I didn't want to take time away from work, but um, I've been learning to bake this week, and wanted to bring you a thank you. For all of you guys here at the shop," she said looking around the room.

It was like somebody rang the dinner bell. Jameson and

Steve practically pounced on the basket as she held it out. Steve pulled back the folded towel on top and sniffed loudly.

"Awww man, Rina, you just stole my heart," Steve said and reached in to pull out the most perfect chocolate muffin I've ever seen. Steve took a huge bite before any of us got a chance to even look inside. "Oh my, this is heaven." He closed his eyes in satisfaction.

That got even Michael walking across the room as Jameson took a bite of some kind of berry tart. "Rina," Jameson said with a muffled mouth full of food. "Oh my, this is the best thing you can give a group of guys that live on nothing but bar food and microwave meals."

Michael reached into the basket that Steve was still holding, took a bite of an enormous cookie and said, "So good. Thank you," and walked back to his station.

I snatched the basket from Steve. "That's mine you Neanderthals. Give it here." I looked into the basket and inside was the biggest assortment of baked goods I'd ever seen. Muffins, cookies, little cakes, and all kinds of things I didn't know how to name. Each looked perfect; each looked amazing.

"What? So many? You have been busy in that little house of yours," I said amazed.

"I found my grandmother's handwritten recipe book. She was well known for baking back in the day. I had to try every recipe in it. I think I've gained five pounds the last three days. I started out wanting to make you cookies but went a little overboard. Now I have so much, I'm going to bring another basket to the coffee shop."

By the time she finished speaking, I grabbed a cookie with coconut, walnuts, and chocolate chips. It was incredible.

If I wasn't sure about Rina before, I was now. The woman could cook.

The room was quiet, nothing but the sound of four happy men devouring homemade food. Rina finally spoke. "So um, yeah, these are for you. I better get going and drop the rest off to Betsy before it gets too late. Are we still on for tomorrow?" she asked me.

"Yup. There's a nice hike to Solomon's Falls that's near you. I'll meet you at your place at eight?"

"Sounds great. I'm looking forward to it."

She smiled at me again, and again my cock stirred.

"See you tomorrow then. I'll leave you boys back to it."

She turned around and walked out. I watched that fine ass of hers until the door closed behind her. I was so in trouble with this one.

Once I heard the rumble of the truck start and tires crunching over gravel, I noticed that the garage was still eerily silent. I turned around to the guys. "What?"

All three of them were staring at me.

"What?" I said, louder this time.

"Dude, if you don't marry her, I will," said Steve as he snatched another cookie and walked back to his station.

"Get the fuck back to work."

17

Rina

I smiled all the way to Betsy's and willed my panties to dry. Holy hell, I think June was right, those men were...sexy couldn't begin to describe the pure male in that room. It was like walking into a den of alpha wolves, and I was Little Red Riding Hood, complete with a basket full of goodies. I smiled to myself at the genuine "niceness" of those guys, for lack of a better word. Even the quiet Viking looking guy, Michael, the type of guy I would normally cross the street if he was walking my way. I knew deep in my gut these were all good men, the type of men I wanted in my corner. I resolved to keep feeding them.

I told Betsy about my baking escapades all during the week. I'd been bringing her in samples to try, and now she was insisting we start selling them in the shop. I brought in a basket early this morning when I went into work, and we had already sold out. She sent me home to get more during my lunch, and that's when I grabbed the basket for the guys over at Singer's.

"Oh, there you are. Thank goodness you made it back in time." Betsy stood opening the door ushering me in.

I looked around at the nearly empty room and asked, "It's not busy, what's wrong?"

"One of those big tour buses just stopped at the corner. Junie called over and said they had some minor maintenance issues, and a bus load of seniors are roaming loose down Main Street. We are about to get hit, hard."

Like preparing for a hurricane, Betsy and I rushed around stocking napkin holders, filling milk, sugar, and creamer, started some fresh coffee on brew and of course stocked the display cabinet full of my baked goods. Thank goodness June ran over to warn us, because when the storm hit about ten minutes later, we were ready.

By the end of my shift, Betsy and I were dead on our feet.

"We killed it today," a tired looking Betsy said, cleaning up tables and loading a huge tray with cardboard cups, napkins, and paper plates. "People are such slobs. I tell you, why can't anybody throw out their own paper cups?"

"I don't know, I always think of seniors as polite and easy, but that was the toughest crowd I've ever dealt with. 'This is too hot, this isn't cool enough, I need a cup of water, no ice dear.'"

Betsy chuckled. I laughed along with her.

"Those old ladies kicked our butt."

"They most certainly did."

"And wow! Girl, we need to do something about your little baking enterprise."

"What do you mean? I'll bake some stuff and you put them in your case." I was happy to bring some baked stuff in. It was like I found an unrealized passion. Baking this past week turned out to be incredibly therapeutic, although probably not on my waistline.

"No, no. It's more complicated than that. You need a business plan. You'll write down your expenses, that includes ingredients, and time to pay yourself. If you actually form a business, you'll be able to write off kitchen expenses too, like wear and tear on your oven and equipment. I want to see all of it."

"Really? You think I can make a legit business baking cookies?"

"Girl, the way not just the town, but that entire busload of tourists, just devoured your inventory, I'd say you have a real good start." She dumped another tray of cups into the trash and turned to me. "We'll do all the math and price out the cost of each baked good. We'll cut in a fee for the shop to sell them, and then you'll profit the rest. I'll help you. Now you're off tomorrow, so when you come back on Saturday, I want to see your homework." She sounded confident and sure this would work.

"Betsy, you'd really help me with this? I wouldn't begin to know how to thank you."

"Thank me? Your baking just doubled our sales this week. Doubled. It's in my best interest as well as yours."

She stopped cleaning and walked toward me. She pursed

her lips together and narrowed her brows, as if trying to decide if she should say something or not.

"Look, I am not one to pry, and you aren't one to share, but I know you need this."

She was standing in front of me now, and I just leaned in and hugged her. I didn't say anything, because tears started forming in my eyes. After a moment, Betsy pushed me off and her eyes were glassy too.

"Ok, go, get out of here. You're making me soft, and I'm not a hugger." She swiped at her eyes. "Draw me up some numbers."

I wiped my eyes too and laughed softly. "I'll get right on it, boss, right after I go hiking with Jesse tomorrow."

"Jesse Singer? The guy that owns the garage and drove you down the mountain? The guy that just 'gave' you a truck?" She leaned in and loud whispered, "One of the sexy vampires June goes on about?"

"He is not a vampire. But yeah, we're friends. He drove me home from O'Dells after the, you know, creep in the hallway incident. We went to his place, and we watched movies."

"You watched movies?" she deadpanned. She stopped and placed her hands on her hips. She didn't believe me, not at all. "That's all?" She shook her head like I just let down all of womankind. "What's wrong with you?" Her voice raised in a whine and laughter. "That," she said, pointing out the door as if he were standing right there, "is one of the finest men I have ever had the pleasure to lay my eyes upon. One of those all American country boy types that every girl in three counties is trying to snag. I wouldn't have lasted five minutes on his sofa before I jumped him." She started fanning herself.

"I'm not his type, and I don't want to *snag* anybody. It's the last thing I need. Look, we both like hiking and old movies. He's nice. We enjoy each other's company."

Betsy's eyebrows raised higher and higher as I spoke.

She finally took a deep, defeated breath and said, "Like I just said, you don't spill your business, but you're coming out of something, something that has you hiding away here. There doesn't seem to be anything wrong with Jesse Singer. Tell you the truth, he seems all kinds of right. But be careful, okay, hon?"

"The last thing I want is a relationship, Betsy. Let's just say you are right in some of it. I'm starting over. I haven't had friends in a very, very long time. It feels good. I'm not the type of woman Jesse Singer is attracted to; I've seen his type of woman. Trust me, I'm not it. It takes the pressure off, ya know? And I want to hike and explore the forests here, and he's willing to show me. But for safety's sake, we are hiking at Solomon's Falls tomorrow. You know, if he turns out to be a serial killer or something." I gave her a wink, grabbed my belongings, and headed home.

18

Rina

"You're killing me here, Singer. How much farther?" I was literally dying in the forest, again. I consider myself in decent shape. I had an elliptical and a treadmill at the city townhouse I religiously used each day. I wasn't allowed to join a gym or God forbid, risk jogging through a park. But this, this was a serious climb. My thighs were burning from the relentless uphill battle I was experiencing. I was out of breath, and I did not bring enough water.

"It's worth it. Trust me. Keep climbing," Jesse said over his shoulder.

At least the view was nice. His ass was fine indeed, and at this point, was the only thing that kept me going.

"I think I hate you." I stopped and leaned against a tree for a moment of rest.

"Almost there, just around this bend." And he disappeared around said bend.

I sighed, pushed off the tree, wiped the sweat from my brow, and followed him. I made it around the bend and when I had Jesse in sight I said, "Seriously, one of your steps is like three of mine. I cannot keep up with you. You're a freaking lumberja—Oh, my God."

Ahead was the most beautiful waterfall I'd ever seen. It might have been the only waterfall I'd ever seen, but it was still beautiful. It was a cascade at least eighty feet up, the clear water rushing from step to step into a large pond. The pond looked so inviting at the moment considering the sweat pouring off my body in this summer heat. I wanted to wade into it, clothes on and all.

"I told you it was worth it," Jesse said, still staring at the waterfall as I walked up next to him.

"That. That is amazing." I couldn't stop staring in wonder. "How did you find this place?"

"It's not well known. The locals like to keep it a town secret. We don't want a lot of traffic, and as you saw, there isn't much of a parking lot. Tourists would just trash it, and then it would be ruined."

"I can respect that. So, it's a secret waterfall."

"Yup."

"Can you go behind it? Is there a cave? Please, oh please tell me there's a cave," I pleaded.

Jesse grinned down at me and dropped his daypack. I followed suit. He grabbed my hand and pulled. "Come on."

I tried to ignore how my body reacted to having his strong hand completely engulf mine as he confidently led me toward the rockface where the water was swiftly cascading.

He walked, I had to jog to keep up. My heart hammered in my chest, and it wasn't because I was exerting myself.

The passage behind the roaring water wasn't easy. Jesse helped me across some surface stones that he easily stepped, but I had to jump. As we got closer to the cliff face, Jesse had to flatten us against the cool wet rocks. The noise was so loud, I couldn't hear anything. Jesse leaned down with an arm snug against my waist to steady me, and his lips near my ear.

"This is the hardest part. Let me steady you and hold on tight."

He placed an arm tight around my waist. I didn't have time to swoon because he pulled me right under and then through the waterfall.

Remember what I said about being hot outside? I take that back. This was some of the coldest water I have ever felt in my life. I was soaked and screaming at the shock of it all. Ice water ran down my body in cold rivulets. I don't think a part of me was spared. Jesse let go of me as soon as we made it through and chuckled at me as I threw my little tantrum.

"You! What did you just do to me?" I sputtered, water shaking off my ball cap as I spoke.

"It's the only way in, darlin'. I told you it was the hardest part." His eyes were still filled with laughter.

"Oh my God. It's so cold." I shook off what I could and then wrapped my arms around myself and took a look around the cave. The light that filtered through the falling water illuminated the cave enough to get a good look around, but it was still dark and damp. The cave wasn't deep, maybe twelve feet wide by twelve feet long, but big enough to walk around the space in a circle. Surprisingly, it wasn't as loud on this side of the water. Maybe because of its dome shape? I didn't know. I saw Jesse walk over and lean against the back wall as he watched me explore.

I turned toward him, smiling. "This is amazing. How did you find out this was back here?"

"I jumped through on a dare when I hiked up here with friends a few years back."

"Wow." I couldn't stop looking around in wonder. The ceiling was ten feet high, and the roaring wall of water crashing down was mesmerizing. I reached my fingers out to feel the water falling like a wall, just a few inches from me. The cave was considerably drier than I thought it would be, but there was still a damp chill in the air, and I was starting to feel it.

We stood there in a comfortable silence for long minutes, circling the cave, and watching the waterfall, me running my hand through it before I turned to him. "Jesse?"

"Yes?" He walked closer to me to hear better.

"Th-th-thank you for bringing me he-here." I shivered, now looking up at him to meet his eyes.

"Shit. Are you cold?" He pushed off the back wall and placed his hands on my cheeks. Clinically, he felt my face, then my hands, and then placed his hands on my shoulders. His beautiful, deep-blue eyes looked down at me concerned. "You're freezing, let's get you out of here."

In that short time, I was shivering uncontrollably. My teeth were chattering, and I could feel my muscles contracting involuntarily. Jesse quickly maneuvered us to the corner of the cave to get ready for the jump out.

"Ready? One, two, three!" and he pulled me back through the water.

I didn't have the energy to scream on the way back out,

but it was just as cold as the way in. The water literally stole my breath away. I was even wetter than before. He didn't bother hopping to the stepping stones. Instead, he walked through the shallow water and hoisted me from one dry stone to the next, quickly and efficiently. Soon, we were at the sunny clearing with our packs.

"Ok, you're going to feel better in a minute." He let go of the still shivering me and rummaged through his pack, pulling out a sweatshirt.

"Take off your shirt," he said.

"What? No!" I managed to grit out.

"Yes. Take off your shirt; you'll feel warmer."

He was still looking at me clinically and detached. I reminded myself that I did not have all of the womanly assets Jesse found attractive, so I got over my modesty and fumbled to get my T-shirt over my head. Jesse took off my cap, helped me find the hem of my shirt and pulled it over my head. He rubbed my bare arms briskly a couple times before lifting my arms and pulling the sweatshirt over my head. He took care to place the hood on and then rubbed my arms again.

Standing incredibly close and looking down with the same care and concern he said, "Good, now, take off your shorts."

"Jesse, if you wanted to seduce me, you could've gone a different route here," I quipped.

"Rina, come on, I'm not thinking of that. Plus, it's not like I haven't seen a woman in panties before."

I felt a little disappointed at that, but I was still feeling resistant.

"You haven't seen me in my panties."

"True, but the sweatshirt will cover you anyway, it's practically to your knees."

"Got a-a g-good point there," I stammered out and took off my shorts.

As I stood there in the sun, I started bouncing up and down to warm myself. Jesse took his own T-shirt off and laid it on the ground to dry. The sight sucked the air right out of my chest. He was beautiful. His well-muscled torso was created from hard days of work, and activities that required strength and endurance. Lean and well defined, his broad chest was taken right out of a fireman's calendar. I didn't think men actually looked like that in real life. A large intricate tattoo covered his entire shoulder front to back and extended down the top of his left upper arm. It was some sort of mountain peaks and trees, but I wasn't close enough to study it. His well-defined chest led down to even more well-defined abs, which then led my eyes to track the perfect V toward—

"Hey, why aren't you taking your pants off?" I asked, breaking myself of the spell I had just put myself under.

Jesse was standing still, watching me watch him. Busted. I was so busted. He smiled, only slightly, as if he were disappointed in me, or didn't know what to do with my obvious thoughts, but still trying to be polite about it. I couldn't read what he was thinking.

"I'm fine. They're a synthetic fabric that will dry in no time. Shouldn't wear cotton pants, ever when hiking for that very reason," he said eyeing my denim shorts. "Come on, let's soak up some of this sunshine."

We laid out on the small sunny clearing and warmed under the perfect blue afternoon sky. We didn't say anything for a long time. I was content to hear the sounds of the water and the forest and feel the sunny breeze warm my body. I removed my socks and boots, and my knees were drawn up with my hands behind my head. I was aware that I was in my panties wearing nothing but an oversized sweatshirt. With my knees bent up, I'm sure you could see my little lacy bikinis, but from all of Jesse's recent reactions, I didn't care that he didn't care. Okay, I cared, but I was determined not to. I wasn't here to get it on with a man I was starting to think of as a friend. I was here because I needed this, and I needed a real friend. And freedom. I needed this freedom to be who I was, and right now I was a simple plain girl hanging out in the wilderness half naked with the most gorgeous man I had ever seen. God help me.

19

Jesse

It took every bit of self-control I had to not pounce on this woman. I don't know how I kept my shit together when she took off her shirt, and I sure as shit don't know how I managed when she wiggled out of those shorts. She was strong with a lean athletic build—not too curvy, but soft and feminine in all the areas that should be. Her plain white bra may have been called practical if I bothered to notice it beyond her perky little tits that would be a perfect fit for my hands. I could see dark nipples, hard and poking through the damp material and my mouth watered. I wanted to get on my knees and pull each one lovingly into my mouth and suck. Her ponytail, now damp, curled around her delicate neck, the soft brown a stark contrast against her creamy pale shoulder. I placed the sweatshirt over her body as quickly as I could and willed my dick to settle down.

Laying on her back with her knees propped up, the sweatshirt barely covered anything at all, and my brain would not stop thinking about those little red lace panties I caught a glimpse of. Red lace panties that led to smooth muscular legs that I wanted wrapped tight around me. My dick was so hard it was throbbing. Thank god my pants were loose enough and my boxer briefs tight enough I didn't give anything away. My self-control was draining by the second, so I stayed on my back, arms above my head and stared at the sky for a long, long time. Rina did not divulge a lot of personal information. I knew there was a story there, and I had a nagging need to know what it was. She was really good at deflecting discussion back to me every time I attempted during the hike. I really wanted to know more about this woman. I turned my head to look at her, resisting the urge to reach out an arm and touch her. "Tell me about you, Rina Sullivan."

"What about me?" She didn't turn toward me and continued staring up at the sky.

"I know you moved here from the city. I know your grandfather died and left you his house. I know you said you wanted a fresh start." I propped an arm up so I could rest my head in my hand. "So tell me, Rina, what did you want a fresh start from?" I know I was treading dangerous water here, but I had to know more.

She turned her head to look at me, one hand shielding her eyes from the sun. "Um, I don't know if I'm ready to share any of that yet."

"What are you willing to share?" I asked.

She didn't answer right away, but then a grin spread across her face. "I love dogs."

"You love dogs?" This is what she wanted me to know?

"Yup. I have this dream of one day owning a dog. A rescue dog, one that was thrown away and needs a family of its own to love, and for them to love him back."

Ok, not what I expected, but also a telling story all on its own.

"What's stopping you?" I asked.

She rolled over onto her side in the grass facing me. Her freckled nose was sun kissed, adding beautiful contrasts to her pale skin and large brown eyes. "Nothing, I guess," she said as if she just came to a revelation. She smiled wide at that point. "Nothing at all. I want to get a dog. I AM going to get a dog." She whooped.

I could see her realizing she could actually do this for herself. I watched the wheels turning in her mind, and the moment she allowed herself permission to have this thing she always wanted. When she realized that nothing was holding her back anymore, it was like watching a flower bloom. It was beautiful to see.

She stood up and felt her clothes for dampness. Deemed dry, she slid her shorts on right in front of me underneath the sweatshirt. She must've realized what she had done, because she turned around next to take off the sweatshirt. My dick, which I finally had under control, stirred to life again as she lifted the shirt over her chest and dropped it on the ground. Her back was smooth, and her waist flowed into the soft curve of her hips. Twin dimples sat above her buttocks at the lower end of her back, and by the time her T-shirt went over her head and covered her up, I was in motion to get my own clothes back on, because if I didn't, I may seriously lose control.

The trip back was uneventful and quiet. By the time we

made it back to the truck, it was late in the afternoon.

"Dinner at my place? I kind of miss cooking real food, not sweets. I'd love to thank you for today, even though you tried to kill me."

"Kill you? How?" I asked, teasing.

"First from exhaustion, and then by freezing." She tucked a piece of hair behind her ear. "But really, thank you. It was a great trip."

"No need to thank me, it was my pleasure. I try to freeze all the girls I take up there." I teased again. "Actually, you're the first woman I've ever hiked with. It was fun for me too. And I will NEVER turn down a home cooked meal. Even my own mother eats out more often than not."

"From what I've seen, you don't really choose to date the outdoorsy type. Breaking a nail and all that," she said, not too kindly.

I detected a bit of disgust, and it was probably because of what she saw of the women at the bar. If I were honest with myself, I could see why. The women I've been known to date have been shallow and high maintenance. I decided to ignore the comment and get back to the subject of food.

"So what's for dinner?" I asked.

"What's your favorite meal?" she asked right back.

I didn't hesitate. "Lasagna."

"You got it, big guy. Swing by the grocery and I'll pick up what we need."

As if watching this gorgeous woman hiking and stripping wasn't enough, Rina in the kitchen was sexy as hell. Clearly in her element, she chopped, mixed, and baked while we talked movies and hiking, and dogs—all safe subjects. When the oven timer dinged, she pulled out the single most decadent lasagna I ever had. I moaned and groaned with each bite. She ate just a small amount but watched me enjoy the meal with pride.

When she served me a third portion onto my plate, she said, "I lived with somebody for five years. I cooked him a meal every day for those five years. Never once did he comment on my cooking. We had guests occasionally that would give me accolades, of course, but I never really knew if my lasagna was as good as I hoped it would be."

I put down my fork. I looked at her, her downcast eyes. I wasn't going to fuck this up, and I was going to capitalize on her willingness to share this crumb of information with me.

"Look at me, Rina." Her big brown eyes lifted to meet mine. I pointed with my fork at the plate. "This is one hundred percent the most amazing lasagna I have ever had. I would gladly, if offered, eat this very meal every day for the rest of my life. And if I had that privilege, I'd thank you every day." I cut off another piece and shoved it in my mouth.

I meant every damn word. When I looked back up, she had tears in her eyes. She quickly went to the sink and asked if I'd like another beer. When I declined, she came back to the table, and we ate the rest of the meal in silence. I know what we were thinking. She was thinking she shared too much and showed me some kind of weakness. I was thinking that I finally got some kind of insight into who she was, and why she struggled to find herself. I knew it was best not to push it, but sooner or later I was going to get to the bottom of who Rina Sullivan was.

20

Rina

Four weeks since our hike to the falls and our first meal together, August rolled in hot, sticky and humid. Jesse and I hiked together every Friday, always ending with dinner at my house. Always ending with a late-night movie, and us practically cuddling on the sofa. Always ending with Jesse leaving, and me crawling into my empty bed, wishing he were with me. He was kind and generous and beautiful, and while I waited with bated breath for him to turn out to be a colossal asshole, he never did.

Thinking that I could simply be friends with Jesse was foolish. Who was I kidding? I was headed for the worst heartbreak of my life, and I never so much as kissed the man. I desperately had to stay away, but I just couldn't.

Luckily, my baking, the house, and work kept me occupied most of the week. Things at Betsy's had changed considerably since I started baking and stocking our display cases. I made cute little labels I ordered online for the pastries, a delicate pink oval with a single gold and etched rose with the words Eleanor Rose's Baking Co. in a flowing script. They were her secrets after all, and naming them after her brought me comfort and made me feel close to the grandmother I never met, and the woman my grandfather loved so completely.

We were selling out every morning, and I was starting to get private orders for birthday parties and large social events. To say I was busy was an understatement. My kitchen had turned into an industrial workstation, and if things kept moving forward like they were, I was going to have to figure something else out. My kitchen was simply too small for the work. For now, I was managing. Fridays with Jesse were the only days off I took.

I was making progress at the house too. Grandpa's clutter was nearly gone, and I only had a few odds and ends to tidy up. I painted the walls and stripped out the carpet exposing the wood floors below. I would have to put off a lot of the outdoor repairs until spring, but they could wait another winter. I was proud of what I had built for myself—my own life, and I was happy.

I started working a later shift at Betsy's so I could bake in the mornings and bring in fresh cookies and cakes in the afternoons, but still it was difficult baking at home and driving back and forth all the time. Betsy was a smart businesswoman. She helped me go through the numbers and we worked out pricing to pay her as well as myself. She thought we both had stumbled on to something and wanted to make it even bigger.

"What do you think of expanding?" Betsy asked me out of the blue one Saturday when we were cleaning up after the morning rush.

"Expanding? Betsy, I can hardly keep up."

"That's what I mean. You've been driving back and forth. Baking mornings and evenings and spending most of your time in between here. I was thinking of installing an oven here, but this place is just too small. I was looking at the empty storefront next door."

I snapped up from cleaning the table to look at her. "What do you mean?" I didn't even come close to having the money to rent something. I was still driving Jesse's truck around. Partly because I didn't have the time and energy to put into finding a decent vehicle, and partly because while I did have some cash, it wasn't enough to get something nice for the winter ahead.

"I was thinking of leasing the storefront next door and putting you in it." She nodded over to the wall that had an empty storefront on the other side.

"You what? Betsy, I can't afford that." I really couldn't with the house repairs I was estimating.

She pulled a chair out and sat. "Hear me out. I know you can't afford it. It would still be my shop. The same owner owns both. If I could convince him to let me take out the common wall and combine the two, we'd have room to put in a kitchen for you. If sales keep up, we'd be able to extend hours and hire more staff. You'd be the owner of Eleanor

Rose, but would lease partial space, fill my displays and cater to private events. It's a win for both of us."

"Wow. You've thought this all out, haven't you?" I said looking around the tiny coffee shop envisioning it twice the size.

"I'm the business lady, numbers are my thing. I'm telling you, this is a good idea, Rina."

"It makes sense, I guess. Are you sure?"

She was already nodding. "I'm sure."

"Let's do it." I beamed.

A broad smile spread across her beautiful face. "I'll talk to the owner and see what I can get him to agree to."

A few hours later, June rushed in. She looked neat and tidy as always. Her makeup was fresh as if recently applied, and her blond bob had not a hair out of place. I could never figure out how some women managed to look perfect all day. June was one of those women.

"Hey, girlfriends!" June announced, pulling out a seat and plopping down.

"Hey, Junie. Long day?" Betsy greeted.

"Don't you know it. Never let me schedule three colorings in a row on a Saturday. I'm wiped."

"Need a drink?" I asked.

"Nothing this place is selling. I need a beer. Or a shot. Preferably both."

"You're out of luck here, best I can do is a double shot of espresso," I teased. "Will have to wait until tonight."

"You're coming with us?" June asked, surprised.

"I am."

"Woot! It's about time we got you back to O'Dell's. Now I'm really looking forward to going."

"We're not letting you out of our sight this time," Betsy said as she passed behind me with a stack of napkins.

"No need for that. You know I'm more of a people watcher, not a dancer. And you ladies," I said pointing first to June and then Betsy. "You ladies like to dance."

"I feel awful about last time." June looked at me as if in apology.

"Don't feel too awful. You know she ended up being rescued by Jesse Singer. They've had a standing date every Friday for the past month."

"It's not a date. We go hiking," I protested.

"Then you make him dinner," Betsy continued.

"It's not a date," I insisted.

"I'd call that a date," June said, sharing a conspiratorial smile with Betsy. "So, you're out in the daylight?"

"He's not a vampire, June." I laughed.

"Just checking." She winked back at me.

21

Rina

I was actually looking forward to having a night out with the girls after the long weeks of work. After spending so much time covered in flour or paint, I wanted to girl it up a bit. That evening, I let my signature ponytail down, my light brown hair curling gently just past my shoulders. I applied a bit of eyeliner and blush along with my mascara. I still wore my usual tight-fitting jeans and boots, but instead of a T-shirt I wore a yellow halter that showed off my flat belly and breasts.

"Damn, girl! You look amazing!" June said when I walked over to the same corner table near the bar where my friends were already seated. She was dressed similar to me, tight jeans and a fitted T-shirt. She added a smokey eye to her already perfect makeup, another trick that was impossible for me to pull off without looking like a raccoon. I made a mental note to ask her for tips because, damn, it looked good.

"Where have you been hiding?" Betsy said, appreciatively eyeing me up and down. Chic and elegant as always, she was wearing a boat neck white blouse with gray slacks that I swear had to be tailored special to fit her perfect vintage movie star figure.

"I was feeling like a little more makeup would do me good. Too much grunt work lately, ya know?" I said smiling at the two of them. There was already a pitcher of beer on the table. June filled a cup and handed it over.

I lifted my drink. "Cheers!"

"Cheers!" they said in unison as our cups clinked together, and we took a drink, settling in to have a good time.

The band was setting up, and the crowd was starting to trickle in. It was getting louder, and I was getting thirstier. I downed my first drink and poured myself another trying to calm my nerves.

Let's be real. I was dressed up because I knew Jesse was coming tonight. I mentioned I'd be here the other day, and he said, "Great! Be there too."

I was nervous. Why? I saw him all the time now. He acted like my big brother and nothing more. He'd ruffle my hair or give me a slap on the back. He never showed signs he was interested. This had disaster written all over it. I was headed for a broken heart.

Much like the last time, Jameson, Steve, Michael and lastly, Jesse, parted the crowd as they walked the length of the large room to the bar. Once again, the crowd pulsed in a collective breath, and once again they were swarmed by women as soon as they settled in. I watched with a curious fascination as Jameson's easy going smile snared three women at once. One snaked an arm around his neck and pulled him in for a kiss. He returned the kiss and turned to talk to another girl. They were jockeying for position, literally, and I had the absurd thought that he would end up taking them all out separately for a good time in the parking lot.

Michael, like me, took a corner spot. He was broody and unsmiling. Everything about him said "Fuck off," but that didn't stop girls from approaching him. He just ignored them until they walked away. He was watchful, I'm certain the guy knew everything happening in the place at every moment.

Steve was leaning over the bar talking to the bartender, Annie. He whispered something in her ear, and she swatted him with her bar towel, flashing a quick smile before reverting to her trademark scowl.

Jesse was facing the room with his elbows backed up onto the bar. He saluted me with his beer when he caught me staring. I saluted back just as I did last time I was here. He started to walk over toward my table when the band started up and my girls started hooting and hollering. The room turned toward the stage and the entire place started hopping, and I lost Jesse in the crowd.

Several songs later into the set, I saw Jesse's ex-girlfriend, Mandy. She was about five foot eight, legs for miles, and wore a leave nothing for the imagination dress, just like last time I saw her. I watched her stride toward Jesse, who was still at his spot at the bar, and watched him watch her, his face unreadable. When they were almost face to face, I turned around. I didn't want to look. I knew Jesse said they were over months ago, but I also knew I hadn't seen or heard of Jesse with any other women, and if Mandy kept coming around all this time, I couldn't imagine any man resisting her if she propositioned him. She sure looked willing.

I threw myself into the music and picked up my empty beer cup. Crap, how many was that? I no sooner set it down before a very fine, yet very young looking man came face to face with me.

"Would you like to dance?" He stuck out a hand for me to grab.

I didn't hesitate. I wanted to push the image of Jesse and Mandy as far out of my mind as I could and this good looking kid was a perfect distraction. "Yes, let's!" I said, and I let him lead the way to where my girls were hopping around like teenagers, and I didn't look back.

His name was Henry. He was barely twenty-one and on the road for work. After our dance he went to the bar and grabbed us drinks, and we yelled into each other's ear for a while. We kept it to easy chit chat: "Where are you from? How do you like this town? What do you do for a living?"

He was a delivery driver for his father's fencing company and on his way across the state to deliver some custom gates. He was very funny and adorable. Harmless. I got a good safe vibe from him. I was having a pretty great time. I may have been a little tipsy, as I drank more than I usually did, but I was nowhere near drunk.

"Another drink?" Henry asked as I finished my last.

"No, thanks. I've had enough. I'm going to have to wait this buzz out for a couple hours, or get June or Betsy to drive me home as it is." The ladies in question kept hitting our home base table between songs to check on me. After I was accosted in the hallway, no way these girls were letting that happen on their watch again.

Henry made it to the bar again for another drink. He handed me a glass as he set down his own. "Just ice water."

"Thank you. This is perfect."

June swung by the table and grabbed Henry by the hand to dance.

"Go." I waved as he disappeared onto the dance floor.

A few minutes later, Henry reappeared, hair mussed and a huge grin on his face. "Those ladies are definite MILFS," Henry said, panting.

I saw the raunchy dirty dance June had just presented him with, and I nearly spit my water. I howled with laughter.

"You've got to tell them that, they will love you forever."

Henry kept his charming smile and said, "Now you, you aren't a MILF, you're too young."

"They're like my overprotective older sisters."

"Who are you calling old?" Betsy said as she swung by the table and lifted the glass of water from my hand to take a drink. She was flushed and panting. She needed the water more than I did at the moment.

"You're a good dancer, Henry."

"Thank you, ma'am. My mother insisted all of her sons learn how to dance. It was humiliating going to dance lessons when I was younger, but I guess it paid off."

"I'd say so!" Betsy said. "Your mama, she's a smart lady. And please, don't call me

ma'am." And she flitted away, back out into the crowd.

I shook my head, smiling at my friend having fun. Heck, I was having fun, a lot of fun. I

caught glimpses of Jesse several times tonight, but we

never quite made it over to each other. I did notice he wasn't with Mandy. I didn't know where she ended up. But it didn't mean there wasn't a steady stream of women circling all of the Singer's crew. Despite wanting to see and talk to Jesse, I reminded myself I wasn't here for him. I was here with my friends, and that was alright.

Henry snagged my attention again. "Hey, Rina, so you work as a barista and bake cookies?"

"I do. Although, I bake more than cookies. I make cake, pies, muffins, tarts, scones—you name it, I bake it."

"So, is that what you were doing today?" Henry had to lean over and talk into my ear.

Except, I didn't hear Henry. The room went to a full buzz as my heart started thumping against my chest, and my ears pulsed with the rhythm. I felt like I was underwater. I couldn't breathe. My glass shattered to the ground, and I sunk down on the floor.

"Rina! Rina, what's wrong?"

I could hear the words muffled from far away. I could vaguely make out that it was Henry, and then Betsy and June.

"Rina? Come on, honey, we're here. You gotta tell us what's wrong."

I could hear myself sobbing and feel tears roll down my face, but I couldn't move, and I was really struggling to breathe. A distant part of me was telling me to snap out of it, but I just couldn't.

Triggers are things from your past that rear their ugly head at times when you least expect it. Triggers can incapacitate you so fast, you don't know what hit you. When Henry leaned over to talk into my ear, like he had all evening, it wasn't him that I heard. It triggered something in my brain and it was Brad's voice leaning in close in my ear, his whiskey breath and his rough hands lifting my dress saying, "*Katrina, what were you doing today?*" And my body reacted, badly.

I heard a bellow from above, "What did you do to her!"

"Nothing, I didn't do anything."

"Move!" Jesse's deep voice boomed, and he was suddenly kneeling in front of me. "I got you, baby," he said as he scooped me up into his arms. He tucked my head to his chest. "It's going to be okay. I got you."

I felt strong arms around me, his lips brushing the top of my head. He pulled me tighter against him.

"I didn't do anything to her, honest," I heard poor Henry say as Jesse carried me out of the bar.

22

Jesse

What the hell? I had no idea what just happened, but when I saw Rina drop to the floor and her friends trying to talk to her, my heart stopped. Seeing her struggling in the corner was one of the scariest moments of my life. She couldn't breathe. Her hands were cramping up from lack of oxygen, and tears were falling down her beautiful face. I saw nothing but her as I stormed across the bar, pushing anybody that was in my way.

I took her outside and sat on the edge of the porch, settling her in my lap. Her body seemed so tiny and fragile curled around me.

"It's going to be okay. I need you to look at me and breathe," I smoothed the hair out of her eyes and tilted her face towards mine. "Look at me, Rina."

She looked up at me, and panic filled her eyes as she struggled for breath.

"Breathe in, breathe out. It's going to be okay."

After a few moments of her focusing on me, her breathing slowed.

"Jesse?" she said in a whisper.

"Don't talk, just breathe. I got you. Nothing is going to happen to you."

Betsy, June, and that little prick they were joking and dancing with all night came rushing out to us. I was going to kill the kid, I really was.

"Oh God, is she alright?" Betsy asked, a hand over her mouth.

"I think it's a panic attack. She's going to be okay. She just needs to breathe her way out of it. Rina, you feeling better?" I felt her hand unfurl and relax on my arms and chest. It reminded me of the panic attacks my mom had when I was a kid, right after my dad left.

"I'm sorry," she said, eyes closing, trying to concentrate on her oxygen intake.

I continued to stroke her hair, soothing her, rocking her.

"What the fuck?" I glared at the three of them. Turning my head to the kid, I said, "What the fuck did you do?"

The kid paled, raised his hands, placating. "Nothing, I swear. We were having a good time. We were just talking and she, she... this happened."

Rina's fingers tightened on my arm and I looked down. She wheezed, "He didn't do anything. He's a nice kid. Please tell him I'm sorry and let him go." She looked at me with pleading eyes. "He didn't do anything."

The kid seemed to hear her and relaxed. Betsy and June just stood by the kid.

"Look, I'm going to take her home. She'll be alright. I'll stay with her tonight to keep an eye on her."

"Please call me with any updates? Rina has my number," said Betsy.

"Me too?" said June.

I agreed, and both ladies kneeled down and murmured concerned goodbyes. Even the kid got close and wished her better. I decided to give the kid a break. Whatever was going on with Rina, it didn't have anything to do with him. He looked mortified and scared, but signaled me a nod, and retreated back inside.

I put Rina in the passenger side of my truck. She was looking much better now and situated herself into the seat. I texted Steve and asked him to let Annie know Rina's truck would be in the lot overnight, and to tell the boys I was taking Rina home. They all wanted to know how she was doing, and I told them she'd fine, she just needed rest.

I kept my hand on her thigh the entire drive, stroking her, trying to soothe her.

"I think I'm better now," she said halfway home and placed her hand on mine and squeezed. "I'm so embarrassed."

"None of that, okay? We'll get you home and some rest."

"That sounds good."

Although I knew she'd be fine, the rest of the ride I was tense. I could feel my jaw working and hoped I didn't look angry for her sake. When we got to the house she insisted on walking, but she was exhausted. I kept my arm around her waist as she unlocked her door and we both walked inside. I took her by the hand and led her upstairs to her bedroom.

"Just sit here, I got this," I said as she sat on the edge of the bed. I lowered to my knees and lifted up each leg gently and removed each boot. Cash and a cell phone fell out as I removed her right boot. So that's why she liked to wear those boots. She watched me and giggled while I scooped up her belongings.

"I can undress myself, you know."

"I know. Let me help." When both boots were removed, I let my hands guide me up over her thighs to the button of her jeans. "Lay back." She complied. God she was beautiful.

She covered her face with her arms in embarrassment, as I helped her wiggle out of her jeans. I turned to the dresser and asked, "Do you have something to sleep in?"

"Second drawer."

I found an old worn T-shirt quickly enough and said, "I'll let you take care of this part yourself. I'll go get some water." And I headed out to the kitchen before she could reply.

When I got down the hall, I let out a deep breath and rubbed my face. What the hell was I doing? This woman was suffering some trauma of I don't know what the hell what, and I couldn't keep my hands off her. I was going to hell for this. My dick didn't seem to care about any of that though. It was hard and throbbing. All I could think of when removing her jeans was licking my way up those soft creamy thighs. Of ripping off those pink panties and placing my cock inside her wetness and fucking her until she screamed my name. I had to get a grip. *This is not the time for that, Singer, you asshole.*

I drank a glass of water myself, refilled it for her, then headed back to her room. She changed into the T-shirt, and I eyed her bra draped over the sitting chair where I had placed her jeans. Great, now I could imagine her bare breasts underneath that T-shirt. *Fuck.*

She was still sitting on the edge of the bed, and I walked to her. "Here. Take a drink."

"Thank you."

She took the glass, drank a sip and placed it on the bedside table. I pulled back the blankets for her and she crawled underneath. I walked to the doorway, turned off the light, and returned to sit at the edge of the bed.

There was no way in hell I was going to leave her alone. I took a deep breath and turned to Rina. I could just make out the outline of her face in the darkness. "I'm staying here with you tonight."

I steeled myself, ready to list all of the reasons I should stay. She was not going to like this. I felt her body shift from under the blankets.

She surprised me by saying, "I'd like that. Thank you."

I exhaled deeply and stripped out of my own clothes, leaving on my boxer briefs, and crawled into the bed next to her. I held her tight, her back to my bare chest. I felt her cry silently until she fell asleep, and my eyes closed shortly after.

23

Rina

I am so humiliated. I can't believe that happened to me last night. It came out of nowhere, that fear. I never had anything like that happen, not even when I was with Brad, let alone a memory of him. The windows were open, and the birds were singing morning songs right outside my window. Light poured in, telling me it was later than my usual wake up time. *The baking!* I had to get my order down to Betsy's. I started to rise, and Jesse's large arm gently laid over me, tugging me back down on the bed. *Oh God. Jesse was in my bed.*

"Where are you going?" his deep timber asked.

"I have to get my baking order down to Betsy," I squeaked, still trying to recover from realizing Jesse was in my bed.

"Done. She stopped by this morning and picked it up."

"She did?"

"Yes. She wanted to check in on you anyway. You were sleeping, but I helped her get the delivery to her car. All is fine. Go back to sleep."

"Oh. Well, I have a lot of things to get done today." I started to rise again.

His arm didn't budge. "You are staying in this bed and resting."

"I can't. I have too much to do." I struggled against him.

"You have nothing to do but lay in this bed, Rina."

I started to speak, but he interrupted.

"Do not insult me with a reply," he grumbled.

"Wow. You aren't a morning person, are you?"

"I like mornings just fine. I just want you to rest. It's important."

"Well, I have to pee. Can I take care of that?"

Finally, he removed his arm. "Okay, but then it's right back here."

I removed my covers and shuffled my way down the hall. I felt like shit. Every muscle in my body ached. I looked longingly at the bath and imagined myself taking a long soak. When was the last time I relaxed like that? I couldn't remember. I used the toilet and then brushed my teeth. That single act alone made me feel a thousand times better. My mind wandered to Jesse, and the tiny little fact he was in my bed, and that seemed so *normal*. I didn't turn to look at him when I got up, but knew he was nearly naked. *In my bed*.

Things weren't feeling so normal now. I anxiously made my way back to my room. Jesse lay on his back, eyes on the ceiling, one arm above his head. The blanket rested at his waist, but his beautiful broad chest was bare to the world. I felt my cheeks get hot as those pretty eyes roved to me.

"Feel better?" he asked. He wasn't quite smiling, but he was clearly amused by my discomfort.

"Much." He patted the space next to him and I crawled back into the bed. He grabbed me and tucked me under his arm, so my head rested on his chest. His arms wrapped around me and he kissed the top of my head. *What. The. Hell?* Since when could Jesse casually kiss the top of my head? Did I black out last night and miss something? My thoughts whirled in confusion around this entire scenario. I didn't get to think for long. I was just so *comfortable*. The rise and fall of his big, warm chest pulled me back into sleep within minutes.

I awoke again, this time to the smell of coffee. It smelled like salvation. I crawled out of bed, pulled on a pair of sweatpants, and made my way down to the kitchen. Jesse's back was to me, hunched over the stove when I shuffled over to the coffee maker to pour myself a mug, and sat down at the tiny kitchen table.

Jesse looked over his shoulder and smiled. "Good morning. Feeling better?"

I grinned up at him over the warm, steamy mug. "I will as soon as I drink this coffee."

"I have the milk and sugar over here if you need it," he said, back still to me.

"None for me. I like my coffee black."

"Really?" he said. "I thought for sure being that you're a barista, you'd want to make it all fancy and shit." He turned around with a cast-iron skillet of steaming pancakes.

"Pancakes!" My stomach immediately let me know it needed food.

"Made from scratch. Google helped. And YouTube." Jesse beamed like he just discovered the secrets to the universe. "I was going to bring it up to you, but you beat me to it."

"It was the coffee. Gets me out of bed every time."

"Ah."

Jesse loaded the rest of the pancakes on to an already plated stack and brought them over. He passed me a plate, fork, butter and syrup. I loaded one onto my plate.

"You are eating more than one." Jesse stared me down.

"It's all I want," I said reaching for the butter, staring right back.

"You've lost weight. Eat."

"I have? And how do you know that?" *He noticed I lost weight?*

"I've noticed."

I thought about it, and I guess it could be true. I've been so busy these past few weeks, I often forgot to eat. Come to think of it, the last meal I remember cooking was our usual Friday night post hike dinner. But then again, it was only Sunday. Had I really not eaten since Friday night?

"Okay, then load me up big guy." He not only added another, but three, totaling four pancakes. I could never eat that. I started to protest, and he growled. I shut my mouth. He smiled and dug into his own plate, stacked eight pancakes high. *Damn.*

He didn't let me clean up the table or wash the dishes. My protesting was useless, although I tried mightily to do so. I was frustrated. It was my house. He cooked; I should clean. I owed him enough as it was, and I felt my debt to Jesse was mounting by the minute. At one point, I grabbed the broom to sweep some flour off the floor. He snatched it from me quick as lightning, and snapped, "Will you just let me take care of you, woman?"

"A man taking care of me is what got me into this mess!" I bellowed back. I snapped my jaw shut in horror, and my hand flew up to cover my mouth. I stood stock still, unable to believe the anger that just tore out of me. Tears sprung up again, and I looked at the floor. My breath started to hitch, and I heard roaring in my ears again. *Not again, please not again.* Jesse dropped the broom and made it across the kitchen in three strides.

He placed his hands on my cheeks, his beautiful dark blue eyes searching mine. I saw concern and sadness. I also saw restrained anger in there too, as they turned an even darker blue than usual, the muscles dancing in his clenched jaw.

"Talk," was all he said.

"I don't want to."

"Why?"

"I can't."

"Why not?"

"Because—"

"Damnit, Rina!"

"Because I'm embarrassed, okay! I lost five years of my life because I was a stupid, stupid girl. Because I am *so angry* at myself for letting some asshole take so much from me, and I didn't even notice. He kept my grandfather's death from me. Can you imagine that? For four months. Four months! I don't think he ever would've told me, but when I found out and confronted him, he beat me so badly I had to hide in a hotel for a week."

I stood there yelling at him, screaming at him. My fists balled tight, my face hot. I wanted to punch a wall, wanted to punch him. I wanted a do-over, to take all of it back. I was a ball of fury and rage, and I didn't know what to do with it.

Jesse didn't say anything for a long time while I breathed out my anger. Finally, he said, "I need to know more. Please. I've been watching you all summer, Rina. You've been running yourself ragged. Working at Betsy's, baking all hours of the day, then starting a business, putting every spare minute into this house, and not letting anybody help. The only break you take is our Friday's together, and even then, you never really talk to me."

He picked up the broom and leaned it against the wall. "I can see you're trying to build something." His eyes were pleading. "I can see you're trying. But you never talk about yourself or your past, and I think it's catching up with you. Please, talk to me. I'm your friend. You know that, right? And I'm guessing right now, you could really use one."

Suddenly exhausted, I slid down the wall onto the floor and put my head in my hands. Jesse slid down next to me. Good. I didn't think I could have talked face to face. I looked straight ahead, staring at the wall when I spoke.

"I don't know who my father is. I never minded. It was what it was. It was always me and my mom against the world. We bounced from place to place when I was a kid, never staying anywhere long. My mom is one of those women who cannot be alone. She always had an endless string of boyfriends. They were almost always decent guys, at least to me, but I don't think a single one of them ever wanted kids. My mom was adventurous, fun, and beautiful, and I always felt I was tolerated as the tag along. Eventually, she'd end the relationship, or they did, and off we would go to start over again.

"When I was around ten, after a particularly bad breakup, Mom packed us up and we came here to live with my grandfather. They had a rocky relationship. I didn't know him before then, and I don't know what happened to bring her home. But I loved my grandfather the moment I met him. We were inseparable. He took me hiking and fishing and brought me around town to meet his friends. I think my mother was trying to show me some stability, or maybe she just didn't have anywhere else to go at the time. So we stayed.

"My mother didn't feel the same. She would leave for weeks, sometimes months at a time. She would come back to visit for a few weeks, meet a new 'friend' and then be off again.

"One day when I was thirteen, I heard my mother and grandfather arguing. I don't know what the fight was about, but I suspected it was about me. My mother came into my room late that night and told me to gather my things. She said my grandfather didn't want us, and we were leaving. My heart broke, of course. I didn't believe her at first, and I didn't speak for a solid month straight. We ended up in Philadelphia. I finished high school and was just about to start my first semester of university when my mom left."

I could feel Jesse turn his head and look at me in surprise. "What do you mean she left?"

I let out a long sigh. "She met *another* boyfriend. His name was Art. Art was divorced with two grown children and he didn't want to take care of another. My mother said she had done her best to raise me, but I was an adult now, and it was time I made it on my own. Next thing I knew, they were gone. She paid the next month's rent on our tiny apartment to 'get me started' and she was gone.

"That was five years ago. I don't know where she is, and I don't really care. She left me like a snake's shed skin and never looked back. What kind of person can do that to their child?"

I looked over at Jesse. I didn't really expect an answer, and I didn't get one. He just put an arm around my shoulder and snuggled me closer to him.

"Tell me more," he said, playing with the ends of my hair.

I leaned my head against the wall. I really didn't want to, but I continued. "I didn't know what to do. I kept enrolled in my classes and got a job at a coffee shop. But I struggled. I had no family; I had no close friends to turn to. I didn't make a living wage, and every moment of my life was consumed with the next step of my survival. Looking back, I was a huge target. Alone, vulnerable, and desperate.

"We had this regular customer, Brad, that came in every morning. He was thirty-three, much older than my eighteen, and a successful lawyer. Over a few short months our little conversations turned into bigger conversations. He asked me on a date. I mean, here was this successful, good looking, older man, interested in *me*. He offered to help me out. I refused, of course, but little things like groceries and a winter coat made me appreciative. Eventually, he asked me to stay with him. He told me he cared for me, wanted to help me. I believed him."

I ran my hands through my hair and leaned my head back against the wall. Jesse gave me an assuring squeeze. I did not want to tell him this. I didn't want to talk about it. I just wanted it to go away. But Jesse was right, it was eating me up.

"The manipulation was so gradual. Looking back, I was so blind, and I'm so ashamed." I let out a small sob. "I can't tell you all of this. It's humiliating."

Jesse leaned over and kissed the top of my head. "You can. It's okay. You have absolutely nothing to be ashamed of. It's going to be fine. I promise."

"I can't."

"You can."

I felt him turn toward me and I turned to look at him. He nodded and signaled a hand to go on.

"Tell me."

"He convinced me I should drop out of school because he could really use the help at home. I'd be able to go back in the future, but he was so busy at work, and after all, he was helping me—why couldn't I help him? So I did. I convinced myself he really needed me, not the other way around. Then it was me quitting my job, then to stop meeting with my friends. I became a willing prisoner, because I did not want to be a burden like I was to my mother and my grandfather.

"He tracked me everywhere I went and questioned where I was if I was 'off schedule.' I was only allowed to go to the grocery. I cooked and cleaned, and um, pleasured him, at every beck and call, all the while telling myself I should be grateful he was taking care of me. He didn't beat me, but the fear of disappointing him, of him telling me I didn't deserve him kept me obedient."

I stopped here and looked at the ceiling, remembering all of the tiny humiliations—a death by a thousand cuts when I didn't even know I was bleeding.

"So what happened?" Jesse interrupted my thoughts. "How did you get to Song?"

"A lawyer arrived at the townhouse one afternoon when Brad was at work. That's when I found out he sent me a letter four months prior and came in person when he didn't receive a response. Brad never told me. It wasn't until that moment, when he told me about my grandfather, a small inheritance, and this house, that it all became painfully clear. It was like being hit with a sledgehammer, and I saw what my life had become.

"When Brad came home, I told him what happened, and I was leaving. He went into a rage. He never raised a hand to me before that, but he beat me then. Over and over, he said he was going to kill me, that I was an ungrateful bitch. I owed him everything, including my life."

I felt Jesse grow still and stiffen. His jaw clenched and his chest was rising and falling like he was taking deep breaths. I looked over at him and his eyes were closed.

I continued, speaking rapidly. I just wanted to get this over with. "I screamed. I tried to fight back. I tried to run away. He never let up; he overwhelmed me. I never had a change to even defend myself.

"A neighbor heard the commotion, knocked on the door and threatened to call the police. Brad left me to answer. I grabbed my bag and went out the fire escape. I ran all the way to the nearest hotel and hid for days until most of the bruising subsided. I ate food from the vending machine, but when I ran out of the small amount of cash I had, I didn't eat at all, too afraid to leave. When I finally got the courage, I cashed the check from my grandfather's estate and it was enough money to buy a car, get myself here and get the lights turned on."

Neither of us spoke for a really long time. I mean a *really* long time. Jesse's tension was palpable. He stiffly removed his hands from my body. The loss of his comfort and warmth was immediate. I looked over at his face, and he was staring straight ahead, his beautiful square jaw tensed and ticking.

My heart sank. He was so disturbed by me and my actions, and I couldn't blame him. Obviously, I had some issues to work out, and this was way more than he signed up for. Jesse finally stood up without saying a word. This was it, I thought to myself, he's going to run, and I will not ask him to stay.

"I can't," he said, never looking at me, and walked out the door.

24

Rina

I couldn't blame him. If the roles were reversed, I'd have done the same. Who wants to deal with that type of baggage? I didn't even bother to look outside and watch him go. I gathered myself off the kitchen floor, and realizing I was still wearing the oversized T-shirt from last night, went back to my bedroom to change. I searched through my dresser looking for a pair of pants, trying really hard not to cry. *You will not cry Rina, you will not*, I willed myself. *You will be fine.* I wasn't convinced. I pushed all the people I cared about in my life away.

"Rina."

The sound of Jesse's voice startled me out of my thoughts.

"Jesse?" I stopped still and stared at him, my heart thudding relentlessly and loudly, fingers shaking. "I thought you left."

He filled my bedroom doorway, each hand on the jam, as if he were trying to stop himself from entering. He looked angry, and sad, and lost, and *unhinged*.

"Jesse?" I asked again when he didn't respond.

He shook his head, as if he were snapping out of something. "I didn't leave. I had a fight with your tree out front."

I looked at his right hand, fingers clenching the wood of the door jamb, knuckles torn and ragged. "What did you do?" I gasped, rushing over, taking his swollen and bleeding hand into mine. "Oh Jesse, what did you do?" I repeated. This was my fault. I needed to fix it.

"We have to clean that up, come on." I led him toward the small adjacent bath where I had antiseptic and bandages. Halfway there, he stopped still. I turned to see his head down staring at the floor. He couldn't even look me in the eyes. I felt the tears start to well, certain I was losing him.

"Jesse?" I said quietly. He peered at me through his long thick lashes. Those pretty blue eyes, darker than I'd ever seen them, locked with mine. I saw rage and sadness and a hundred emotions in his gaze. Before I was able to process what was happening, he tugged me to him, and his lips came down on mine.

It wasn't a soft kiss. It was frantic and desperate, hungry and devouring. I wanted, no *needed*, to get closer. I moved into him. One of his arms wrapped around my waist, the other to the back of my head, and he pulled me even closer to his strong, warm body. His scent enveloped me, a heady mix of wood, oil, and man. My mouth opened for him, our tongues exploring, searching, tasting. I could feel his need coursing through all parts of him, and my body answered. I was lost. I was completely and utterly drowning in desire.

He walked me back until the backs of my knees hit the bed, and I was forced to sit down. He broke the kiss, got down on his knees in front of me and looked straight at me with his hands now cupping my face, eyes searching.

"I don't want to be your friend anymore, Rina." His voice was low and throaty.

"You don't?" My heart was thudding so loudly, I could barely hear myself.

"Nope." The corner of his mouth lifted slightly.

"Why not?" I couldn't look him in the eye any longer and tried to look away.

He gently lifted my face and placed his forehead to mine. "I've tried everything I could to be friends, and I can't do it anymore. I want you. I want every part of you, and I'm tired of trying to stay away. I'm an asshole for doing this, at this moment, right after you told me all that you've gone through."

He leaned back to look at my face, his thumbs unconsciously rubbing the inside of my bare knees. "I know you needed this time, to find your way, to create a new beginning, but when you told me what happened, something inside snapped. I know exactly what I want."

"And that is?" I asked, my own hands shaking.

"I want to seriously fuck up this Brad guy." He snarled. "I want to find your bitch of a mother and rip her to pieces and tell her what a fucked up person she is. But, most of all, I want to lean you back on this bed, crawl over the top of you, and make you mine a thousand different ways."

"Oh." I exhaled. I wanted to say so much more, but I couldn't breathe, let alone speak. I wanted this, right? He was thinking of me as much as I was thinking of him? *Holy shit.* I gripped him by his forearms, pulling him up and toward me. "Ok, let's do that last one then."

He leaned forward and trailed that beautiful mouth down my neck and across my collarbone. His tongue was doing magical things to my neck as he traveled downward. He let out a groan of frustration when he reached my shirt, but he lifted me, and I helped him pull the shirt over my head. I lay back down on my bed in only my bra and panties. Heat filled his gaze as he looked upon me, his eyes lazily roving the length of my body.

With a long exhale he rumbled, "You are so beautiful, and you don't even know it."

I didn't know what to say to that. I mean, *I was?* I wasn't about to think too hard on it. My body needed this man in ways my brain hadn't comprehended yet. But looking up at him fully clothed, when I was not, I knew I wanted his bare skin next to mine. "Take off your shirt."

He did so without another word, and soon he was looming atop me. Lust and desire radiated from him as I gazed over the length of his body. My hands reached out to touch him, roaming greedily as if they weren't able to touch him enough. He watched me as my hands caressed the hard plains of his chest and stomach and then reached around his back and pulled him toward me.

His wicked tongue trailed down to my breasts. He grabbed one breast in his hand, and the other he grazed with his mouth over the top of my bra. I let out a desire filled moan, giving him permission to pull down my bra exposing my painfully hard nipple. He pulled it into his mouth, and sucked gently, while caressing my other with his thumb. I gasped again in pleasure as he repeated the act with the other, this time sucking harder, nipping and tugging. Somehow, my bra fell away as I moaned in delight.

I reached down to fuss with the button of his jeans, his massive erection evident against me and I had a sudden and overwhelming desire to have his cock in my hands. He leaned back and stood at the side of the bed. With his help unbuttoning, I pushed down his jeans and boxer briefs together and his cock sprung free of its restraint. He pushed his clothing down and stepped out of his pants. His cock stood at attention in front of me, long and thick. The swollen head beaded a drop of precum, and I licked my lips and looked up at him as I took him into my hands. I wrapped one hand around his shaft and the other reached down to feel the heavy weight of his balls. Jesse let out a soft growl, and I smiled up at him and went to lean in. His hands grabbed both of mine. He pushed me onto my back, and held them over my head, pushing them into the bed.

"I'm ready to come now. If you do that, we won't get very far," he growled into my ear. "I've wanted you so badly, I'm ready to explode. Let me explore you." He covered my mouth with his once again, his tongue exploring me with a frantic desire.

He shifted his hands so that one of his held both my wrists in place over my head, and the other explored my body. His hot mouth caressed my nipples again. He nipped and sucked and pulled, while I arched into him wanting more. He let go of my hands and tugged off my panties. Sitting up as he pulled them slowly down my legs, his eyes roamed my body, his hands following. He pushed up one knee, then the other, and stared down at my wet pussy.

"This, I want this," he said as his head dipped between my legs.

Oh. My. God. If I thought he was doing amazing things to me before, I was wrong. His tongue flicked out against my clit, and I let out a deep moan.

"So sweet. You taste so sweet," he said and went on a full on attack as he lapped at my juices, down my core, and back to my clit. His hand reached up and squeezed a nipple, just as his other hand plunged first one, then two fingers inside me.

I screamed, an orgasm ripping free from my body so fast and so hard, I was unprepared for the tidal wave of pleasure coursing through me. "Jesse!" I squeaked out, my pussy contracting around his hand as he continued to tongue me over and over until the wave subsided.

"You like that, baby?" he said looking up at me from between my thighs. He wiped my glistening wetness off his short-bearded chin as he rose once again above me.

"I've never come like that...oh God." I paused, not wanting to tell him I've never had a man give me an orgasm before, suddenly ashamed. Instead, I continued. "I want you inside me." I was thinking of nothing else but his cock buried deep within me.

"Oh no, not yet." He smirked. "I'm not nearly done with you."

"Please," I begged. "I don't think I can take any more."

He smiled as he crept back up my body like a predator. He smashed his mouth on mine and I tasted myself on his tongue. He broke free of this kiss and said, "Not until I taste every single part of you," and he lazily kissed my neck and made his way back down to my breasts. When he reached my thighs again, my body was screaming with need.

He reached into his jeans pocket on the floor and produced a condom. I greedily snatched it out of his hand and ripped it open.

"Me," I said breathlessly as I sat up and took his cock in my hands. I pulled out the condom and stroked the long hard length of him, then I leaned forward and kissed the swollen head. I tasted the salty fluid on the tip of my tongue, and I wanted more. I flicked out my tongue and licked along the slit of his penis, then opened my mouth to take him whole. My mouth covered him as he entered the back of my throat.

"Rina."

That sexy growl made my stomach flip in anticipation. He grabbed me by the hair and gently pulled me off of him.

"I told you, I won't last two seconds if you do that. I've wanted this for so long." He reached between us plunging two fingers deep inside me. Pushing in and out until my eyes rolled back in my head and my hands dropped to my sides.

"Jesse!" was all I could get out, before he took the condom from my hand and rolled it on.

He loomed over me again and positioned himself at my entrance. When I felt the tip of him enter me, we both moaned as he slid deeper inside. When he was fully seated, he paused a moment before pulling out, slowly, oh so painfully slowly. I wanted more, I needed more, and I reached around, grabbed his hard tight ass, and pushed him toward me, my hips rising to meet his. He pumped in and out of me at first slowly, then steadily faster and faster. I felt myself building again.

"More," I said, and he drove into me hard, like a machine. I looked up to see his face, his beautiful blue eyes bore into mine, and I couldn't look away. I felt the heat gathering again. It was torture, but I wanted it to last forever.

We moved with each other, me meeting him thrust for thrust until my body couldn't take any more. I screamed again as the orgasm crashed over me, a hot molten wave of pure pleasure, coursing over and over as he continued to thrust deep into me harder and harder. His rhythm grew frantic and out of control, his own pleasure taking over until he roared his release into me.

———

We spent the rest of the morning in bed. I can say with certainty, it was the best day of my life. I never wanted to leave this bed. I never wanted to leave him.

"I'm such an asshole," Jesse said, staring up at the ceiling as I curled up next to him.

"What! Why would you say that?" I just had the most amazing sex of my life. I was not going to let him bring me down.

"Because, you don't need this right now. This complication, I mean."

"You want to call this a complication?" I said pointing a finger into his chest. "I'll have you know, I love this complication. Plus, I think you're pretty good at knowing what I need. How the hell you got this wrong, I'm dumbfounded. I've never had amazing sex like that. I've never had anything close to that."

"I have been pretty good at it so far." He smirked. I playfully swatted him.

"Yes, you have. More than good. Fantastic. I need this. I

need you. I need you to never leave this bed. At least for the next few hours. And I'll be needing you to come back and do it again, okay? On a regular basis."

He smiled, that big, beautiful grin. "Your wish is my command."

"Plus, I'm the one that should be apologizing," I admitted.

"This is getting ridiculous." He turned his head to me. "Why do you need to apologize?"

"I'm a train wreck. All you do is rescue me! You rescued me from a bear in the woods, you rescued me by giving me a truck to drive, you rescued me when I had an anxiety attack in a bar, which is the most embarrassing moment of my life by the way, and now you just rescued me from my vibrator, which I thought was the only thing that could give me an orgasm. Now it's a disappointment; I don't think I can ever use it again."

"You have a vibrator? Can I see it?" He looked around the room, wide eyed and amused.

"Yes, how else am I supposed to orgasm? And no, you can't see it. It's dead to me now anyway."

"Wait, are you saying you've never had an orgasm? Like during sex?"

Shit. I didn't want him to figure that out. But if we were going to have a relationship, I wasn't going to start out lying. "No, I haven't. Can we leave it at that? Please?" I rolled over, plopped my head on the pillow and covered an arm over my face in embarrassment.

He rolled on top of me, removing my arm so I was forced to look at him. All amusement gone, he said, "Let me make this clear to you right now, Rina Sullivan. You do not need rescuing. You are smart, resourceful, and brave. Probably the bravest person I've met. Yeah, I've had opportunities to help you, but you sure as shit didn't need me. Believe me, I know insecure, needy women. When somebody comes to you each day wanting something from you, asking to be rescued every single day, that is not the same thing as helping somebody out because you can."

I looked at him thoughtfully, trying to figure out what he was saying. "You're talking about Mandy?"

"Yes, Mandy." He rolled off me, and now it was his turn to stare at the ceiling. "She thinks she was given a raw deal being born here. She thinks her only chance is to bag somebody successful and take what they have." His hand caressed my thigh, and he rolled over to face me. "You. What have you ever asked me for? Nothing. I've offered you things that could help, but you were already doing it your way, not crying or complaining."

"But I—"

"Did you ask me to paint this house? Nope, you went ahead and did it yourself. Did you ask for a car? Nope. You solved your own problem by getting a bike. You never once complained about it. You saw opportunity with your baking and acted upon it, trying to improve yourself and your situation."

"I have to give Betsy credit for that."

"The point is, I don't see you ever blaming others for anything in your life. You walked in this town with nothing, and now you're starting your own business. Believe me, I think you're rescuing me, more than you know."

"How the heck am I rescuing you?"

"I told you. Women always want something from me. They make me feel guilty for having what I have. This is a small town without a lot of opportunities. I don't have much, but by those standards I've got more than most. I've worked hard for that shop, Rina, and I always felt guilty for owning it. You know why? Because before you, I thought I had to take care of everybody. Jameson, my mother, and even Mandy. I love my mother and Jameson. I help them because I want to. I have something to offer them, and it makes me happy to see them happy. The same goes for you. It makes me happy. Simple as that. Mandy is a terrible person who uses anybody she can to try to get ahead. She thinks of nothing but herself and what others can do for her."

"Yeah, but look at her, even you have to admit to me she's beautiful. I couldn't hold a candle to that. And to be honest, I'm very insecure about it."

"Beauty is only skin deep. I look at her and all I see is ugly, inside and out. You're beautiful," he said caressing my cheek. "The most beautiful thing about you is you don't even realize it. I will never get enough." He leaned forward and kissed me gently. "I think you are amazing, strong and brave. I've thought of nothing but being in this bed with you for two months. How did you not see that?"

Oh boy, really? We kissed again. His lips roamed down my neck and behind my ear. I could forget this conversation and let things keep moving, but I wanted to know more about Mandy. It was petty of me, I know. He obviously had feelings for her at some point, and I was jealous. "So, what happened with you two?"

He relaxed onto his back and let out a deep breath, "She lied to me about being pregnant and tried to get me to marry her."

That got my attention. I rolled over, propped my elbow,

and placed my head in my hand. I looked at him incredulously. "She what? No way?"

"The sad thing? I would have if things didn't fall apart for her."

"What happened?" Seeing the tension in his body, I reached out to gently glide my fingers down the inside of his arm.

"When she told me she was pregnant, I was suspicious. I always used a condom, always. Even after being with her for so long. But I wanted to man up and do the right thing too. She showed me the positive pregnancy test, so I believed her. We started looking for houses together. The apartment was apparently too small, and Mandy convinced me that the garage wasn't a place to raise a baby. I was just about to go into massive debt to purchase a house I couldn't really afford because she convinced me the baby needed it." He shifted on the bed to sit up, legs hanging over, elbows on his knees. "I never loved her, not even close. I was feeling used for a long while by that point and tried to end things several times. She always wanted something from me—new clothes, new car, money for a haircut, a manicure."

I looked down at my own weathered hands with their rough cuticles and calloused palms.

"She hardly works," Jesse continued. "A few shifts at The Diner when they need an extra server. She's never tried to do more, just enough to get what she wants. But every time I tried to end it, she would freak. Saying she wasn't given the same opportunities. That she loved me, that her life would be over without me. It was ridiculous looking back, but I felt obligated, you know?"

I nodded. I did know. "So, you didn't give her all she wanted, so she faked a pregnancy?"

"She didn't fake the pregnancy part. Just that it was mine."

"Shit." I blew out a breath and let it hang there a second, before I waved him on. "Explain."

"Like I said, I always used a condom. I guess deep down inside, I knew she wanted to get pregnant, if only to trap me into a marriage. So, I'm at work one day thinking I'm going to be a dad, and stuck in this loveless relationship, and soon to be in massive debt. Seriously, Rina, I was freaked out thinking I fucked up my life."

He blew out a deep breath and looked at the ceiling. "This guy comes into the garage. He says he's from Castor, and he needs money. I'd never seen the guy before. He's jittery and jumping around looking all paranoid. He's probably eighteen or twenty years old. Dumb young kid, greasy hair, and an overall creepy motherfucker. I tell him I don't know who he is or what he's talking about. He goes off saying that Mandy owes him for the baby. I'm really confused at this point. I don't know what to think."

He looked at me, sadness etched deep in his eyes, and took a deep breath. "This is the part that is going to freak you the hell out. Mandy had fucked this guy for weeks. She told him her boyfriend was sterile, and they were trying for a baby but couldn't have one together. She told him the fuck was free, no strings attached. I guess the guy ran out of drugs or something, I don't really know, and tracked me down thinking I'd pay him for his sperm or something. She went far out of her way, out of town even, to find this guy."

"Oh my God." I grabbed his hand and squeezed.

"That's not the end. I'm calm as can be. I tell the guy sure, let's go for a ride and find Mandy. We drive over to her at her parents' house, and I bring the guy to the front door. When she opens the door, she turns white as a ghost and I can see it in her eyes. This guy is telling the truth, and I'm a sucker. All I say is, 'Your baby daddy is looking for you,' and I turned around and walked away."

"That's one of the most screwed up stories I've ever heard," I said. "So, what happened to the baby?"

Jesse's voice got real low, and an angry glint stared back at me. "Apparently, she lost the baby a few weeks later. She called me, crying and hysterical. She still called it 'our' baby. She thought she lost the baby because of what she did. I tried to get her to go to a counselor, even offered to pay for it, but she refused. She called me an asshole for leaving her, and that was the end."

My hand was over my mouth in shock. "That's terrible. She's sick. Jesse, she has to be a sick person to do all of that."

"I agree. She's messed up. I didn't want that baby at first. But after a while when I thought it was mine, I was starting to like the idea of being a father. I think I'd like to be a dad someday and she tainted that for me. Here's the truth. If I did end up marrying her and raising that baby, and later found out it wasn't mine, I would have still loved it. I know I would."

That I knew for sure. That's just who he was. "Oh Jesse, I'm so sorry." And I meant it. I was horrified. What a terrible thing to go through. What a fucking bitch. "So you want children?" I asked.

"Yes, lots. Like five or six of them."

"Five or six! You're crazy!" I practically screamed but laughed.

"Do you want children?" Jesse asked.

"Maybe one day," I said.

We both knew it was too early to have a conversation like this, so we didn't say anything for a while. Jesse pulled me down, and we laid in silence, each of us running our hands down the other's body. It felt so right, and so perfect, in that bed, in his arms. I never wanted it to end.

"I think we need to stop conversing." He leaned over and kissed me.

"You do?" I grinned when I broke our kiss.

"Mmmmm. Let's do this instead." He bent down and pressed his mouth to mine again, and I was lost.

Yes, please.

25

Jesse

We spent the rest of the morning lazing around my house into mid-afternoon. We didn't discuss much more of me, my past or the last twenty-four hours. I think he sensed I was pretty tired of the rehash, and he really wanted me to take a break. We didn't talk about the screwed up Mandy situation either. We were both ready to move on.

"I think you should take tomorrow off too," Jesse said while we polished off a carton of Rocky Road ice cream while still lying in my bed.

"No way. I couldn't do that to Betsy. I have goodies to bake, people are counting on me."

"I could help. I made pancakes today. That makes me qualified." He grinned.

"Really, I can do it. I like to bake. It's relaxing. It's good for me." It was true. I'd found my calling. I enjoying making sweets for people. Their smiles always brought a smile to my own face.

Jesse suddenly hopped up, eyes bright and full of mischief. "Come on, we're going somewhere."

"We are?"

"Yup. I have an idea."

"Where?"

"It's a surprise."

As much as I hate surprises, I didn't push it. He looked so excited and happy, I couldn't deny him. We loaded into his truck and off we went down the road.

We drove for a good thirty minutes. I kept making guesses and he wouldn't give me a clue. Eventually, we pulled into a parking lot with a nondescript cinder block building at the end. In utilitarian block letters affixed to the building were the words, "Castor Animal Rescue."

"You took me to the animal shelter!" I just about exploded.

"I sure did. You, my lady, need a dog." He pointed at me.

"I do?"

"You do. You need a friend, now that *I'm* not your friend anymore."

"I do. Damn right I do." I beamed.

26

Rina

The animal shelter was one of the saddest places I'd ever been. Rows upon rows of dogs in runs lined the corridors. I learned this particular shelter was where animal control brought dogs and cats that were not only strays running loose on the street, but abuse and neglect cases. The variety of animals was astounding. I had no idea.

Jesse and I walked up and down the aisles looking at all the poor creatures. Most dogs had been through this before. We were like a couple of prospective parents looking for a new child. The dogs would run to the front of the cages, bark loudly, paws catching on the chain link, as if to say, "Please pick me!" They'd jump up and down, and spin around. It was loud and smelly and awful, and I wanted to take every single one home with me.

I didn't really know anything at all about dogs. Jesse told

me the right one would call to me, and he did. At the end of a particular aisle, a dog sat in the corner, looking forlornly at the two of us. He didn't stand up and bark like the other dogs. Instead, he tracked our movements thoughtfully. He was a medium size dog, gray and black. Half his face and one ear was black, while the other a mottled gray. He looked like a mutt. He looked just like the dog from the original *Mad Max* movie, and I instantly loved him.

"Blue Heeler," one of the attendants said as they walked up to us and heard me call the dog a mutt and reference the film. He was a gangly six foot tall redheaded kid with a face full of freckles and pimples. His name tag said "Barry." He seemed to genuinely love the animals and made an effort to help us with a good match.

"Oh, I've never heard of those," I said. "What are they like?"

"Nice dogs, loyal, with a lot of energy."

"He doesn't seem to have a ton of energy." I looked at the poor dog who appeared to shove himself as far into the corner as possible.

"I don't think he knows he can use it. Animal Control seized him a few weeks ago. He's only about two years old but spent his entire life on a three foot chain outside. Animal control went to investigate, and the owner surrendered him to us. I guess the guy thought it was easier to give the dog up than put in the energy to provide him with an adequate home. That happens a lot," Barry said, kneeling in front of the kennel looking at the dog.

"That's awful."

"It is. But we have him now, and that's better than where he was. So, do you want to take him out and meet him?"

Barry explained that they liked to put people and dogs together in a yard to see how they got along. If he saw it wasn't a good match, he would let us know.

"Yes, let's do it."

Barry produced a leash and opened the gate. The poor dog backed into the corner and seemed to try to shrink himself smaller, though he didn't do anything when the leash was put on. He stood stock still, a worried look on his cute face. Barry led the dog to a large pen without incident and put us and the dog inside. He unhooked the leash and said, "Hang out here for a while and get to know him." And he walked away.

Jesse and I looked at each other. We obviously didn't know what to do. I felt a sudden surge of panic at the loss of Barry. The dog scrambled to get away by fleeing toward the edge of the pen and stuck his head in the corner, facing away from us. He didn't move. It was heartbreaking. I decided to just go with my gut and do whatever felt right. I walked over and sat on the floor next to him.

"Hey there, boy," I said and patted the ground next to me.

The dog turned around cautiously but didn't seem interested in me at all. I did notice that he kept a wary eye on Jesse though.

"Want to meet me? Let's be friends," I said in a sing-song voice. Nothing from the dog. Jesse came over to sit next to me. The dog turned, crouched low and bared its teeth.

"Whoa there, doggie. I'm not going to hurt her." Jesse, moving slowly, placed a hand on my thigh. We looked at each other and smiled worriedly. We were both a tiny bit scared. The dog, now facing us, didn't move.

I looked at him again, "Hey there, boy. Aren't you a pretty

boy? I bet you'd like to go on some hikes with us. Yes, you would, I can feel it. You're a hiking dog." I kept on with that sing-song voice, and after a while the dog thumped his tail once and laid down.

Jesse and I started chatting with each other for a while, sometimes asking the dog questions. Eventually, his ears started perking up when acknowledged. I patted the space next to me again, and this time not only did the dog come over, he crawled right into my lap and curled up. It was like he said, "I pick you too." Jesse reached a hand over and pet the top of his head, and the dog leaned into my chest. That was the moment we knew this was the dog for me.

We spent more time in the pen getting to know the dog that Jesse started calling Mad Max. "Max" had decided I was his person and stuck to my heels like glue. Not sure if that's why they called them heelers, but it sure felt like it.

Barry was ecstatic. You'd think a kid like that would be pretty blah, but he was a genuine animal lover. "I knew it. I knew it! I've had other people take a look at that dog, and really want to take him home because he's a purebred, and for some reason folks think that's important. It's not," he said to me conspiratorially. "But they weren't good fits. I wouldn't let him go. The moment I saw you sitting on the floor, I knew. Congratulations, looks like Max here has picked his person."

And that is how I got myself a dog.

27

Rina

The next few weeks buzzed by. The evenings were becoming cooler, and the leaves were just beginning to change color. Betsy and I were moving steadily forward with our plan to conjoin Betsy's Coffee and Eleanor Rose's Baked Goods. We weren't able to get approval to bust the wall between shops, but the owner did let us rent the adjoining space, and also approved a doorway between the two. He reasoned it could be put back to rights easily if things didn't work out. Betsy was already working on purchasing the two units, but for now, the owner wasn't budging. Knowing Betsy, she'd own the entire strip of storefront on our block before long.

I woke early to bake at home each morning and cleaned up the dusty old rental space after I delivered the baked goods, as well as working my shifts at Betsy's. By the end of the first week, Betsy had two industrial ovens delivered. Jesse recruited the guys from the garage to help him install cabinets, shelving, and sinks. I scoured the thrift shops for art to cover the walls. It wasn't anything fancy, but we managed a few mismatched tables, which added to the charm, and all of the necessities to start working from Main Street rather than my house.

It was hard to believe only three months ago I had nothing. No friends, no family, no job, and no home. Now I was going to be a business owner, had an incredible man I was head over heels for, great friends, a home, *and* a dog. It seemed too good to be true, but Jesse kept telling me it was my determination and hard work, nothing else.

Betsy was incredible with business and finance. We had worked the numbers over and over, and she assured me that we'd be successful, and Eleanor Rose's recipes would soon be famous in the tri-state area. Her enthusiasm was infectious.

Despite seeing her nearly every day, Betsy and I hadn't had much of a chance to talk. Honestly, there hadn't been much opportunity. I wasn't keeping anything from her, we were all just really busy. The first day Jesse came in to help with the cabinets, he grabbed me from behind and kissed my neck. Betsy gave me a knowing smirk, and I smiled wide back at her. That had been it until we had a slow moment in the coffee shop late one morning. June stopped by to chat before her next client, and we sat down to share a cup of coffee and catch up.

"So, you and Jesse? Like I didn't see that coming," Betsy asked grinning over her coffee cup.

"Ok, Rina, you have to spill. You and Jesse have been

steaming for months now. It was only a matter of time before that kettle whistled," June chimed in.

"Really, I didn't see it at all. I thought we were friends. I had no idea he was attracted to me. Honest." I leaned over and gave Max a pat on the head. Forever under my feet, he pushed his head into my palm.

"Isn't that right, Max?" I said to him, and his tail thumped once on the floor. I had brought him to work all week. I wasn't sure if it was allowed or not. Betsy had welcomed him, and that worked for me. Until somebody complained, Max was staying with me.

I looked back up at the girls and continued. "And then the morning after my anxiety attack at the bar, he said he didn't want to be my friend anymore, and he kissed me."

"I'm swooning! He actually said that?" June squealed. It was so like June to use the word "swooning" and I chuckled.

"He did."

"Rina, that's so romantic. Being old and married, I have to live these things through others," Betsy said, eyes bright and smiling.

"Stop it! You are not old. And your husband is a fine looking man, if you don't mind me saying so," I returned.

"My Lou is handsome, it's true, But Jesse Singer? That man is smoking hot. I have no idea why he hasn't been snatched up before now," said June.

"Well, you've seen his ex-girlfriend, Mandy," I said, casually.

"Oh yeah, I saw them at O'Dell's sometimes. She seemed like a nasty piece of work. Beautiful, but so was Lucifer," Betsy said.

"I've heard she's turned really nasty. Wasn't always that

way—she seemed like a nice enough girl when she was with Jesse. But since they broke up? I've seen her hanging on any man that'll stick out an elbow," June said.

"June Ortega!" Betsy scolded.

"It's true. I heard it from Lou. He's had run-ins with her before."

"It's true. She's all those things, so I'd stay away from her. She's scary." I didn't want to tell Jesse's story to the girls. It seemed too personal. Instead, I redirected. "He's so hot. So hot. I can't keep my hands off him. I can't believe I'm even gushing like this. And not only that, he's so genuine." I gripped the paper napkin in front of me and started tearing at the edges. "To be perfectly honest, I'm terrified. I'm waiting for the other shoe to drop, you know what I mean? Like this cannot be real. Things this good don't happen to me."

"Oh, honey, they can, and they do. You just have to seize those opportunities. Jesse Singer seems like a genuine nice guy. What are you scared of?" asked Betsy.

"That he'll figure out who I really am?" I admitted.

"And what is that?" This coming from June as she bent down to sneak Max a piece of her muffin. That dog was going to get fat if he kept hanging out here with me. I didn't have the heart to leave him home, unless I absolutely had to. Betsy liked having him around too.

"Not what he wants? I don't know. I'm just terrified. My last relationship took a lot from me. I'm just starting to find myself again. Things with Jesse have moved really fast. Too fast. I don't know how to slow it down. I don't know if I want to slow it down."

"Why do you think this is moving so fast? You two have

been hanging out for months, mooning over each other. Everyone could see it." Betsy took a sip of her coffee.

"Everyone?" I asked.

"Everyone!" they both said in unison.

"Of course, when you two collided it was going to move fast." Betsy fanned herself. "Oh, my heavens, it's getting hot in here." Betsy smirked.

"Maybe because he's *the one* and when you know, you know." June smirked right along with Betsy. They were both staring at me with stars in their eyes.

"You do?"

"Well, that's what I've read in romance novels. I don't really know. I had to talk myself into marrying my husband. I should've taken that as a sign and waited for the real thing," said Betsy.

"It was real for me. When Lou and I got together, I knew," June confirmed.

"That's just it. How do I know it's the real thing? I'm so confused." I leaned my head back and let out a deep sigh.

"The heart wants what the heart wants. I don't think there's a way to stop it. I think when you decide to fight for it or sacrifice for it without a single moment of thought or hesitation, that's when you know," June advised. "When you're ready to throw yourself in front of a train for them, and they you, that's love."

Max was my constant companion, and I couldn't imagine him not being in my life. He followed my heels everywhere I went. I had to kick him out of the bathroom so I could take care of my private business, and even the bedroom when me and Jesse were together.

Not that I had any experience with dogs, but I swear he was the smartest dog in the world. Within three days of coming home, he learned the English language, and understood every word I said. Like one day I was at the shop and I misplaced my phone. I looked over to Max and said, "Where's my phone, Max?"

Max got up and trotted around the space. I heard a soft yip and when I walked over to him, he was standing in front of the sink, looking down at my phone where I must've dropped it.

"That's kind of creepy," Betsy had said when she walked past.

"I think he's the smartest dog in the world." And I believed it.

Max loved hiking, and Jesse and I took him out on a nightly walk, and a long hike on our days off to make up for those years he was stuck tied to that chain. He bounced up and down the trails exploring ahead and running back. Jesse bought him a red bandana to tie around his neck, and he looked like a proper hiking dog. When Jesse and I stopped to take a rest, he'd sit in front of us and whine, "Let's go! Let's go!" and then his heeler instincts would kick in and he'd start circling us, herding us to keep moving. Barry was right, he hadn't known he could run around, because now that he was a hiker, the dog never quit.

But when I was at work, he knew it was down time. Betsy put a large dog bed behind the counter for him, and there he stayed for my entire shift. He didn't look at or bother another human, just waited for me to say, "Let's go

Max!" and he would spring into action and hop into the truck.

Jesse and I couldn't keep our hands off each other. We'd been spending nearly every night together at my place. Apparently, Jameson liked this development because he had the apartment to himself. He was leaving to go back to school in three days for one last semester. He'd be home by Christmas complete with a college degree.

Eventually though, Jesse admitted he had some work to catch up on and the hours helping me and staying with me had been pushing back the work he wanted to get done at the shop.

"What? Why didn't you tell me?" I felt guilty. He was doing too much, and I, the selfish person I was, didn't even think about that.

He grabbed me by the waist and nuzzled my ear. "It's no big deal, I'd rather be here licking all over your body, making you scream."

"Stop it!" I tried to push him off, without success. "You can't neglect your work. You love working on your restorations. I still have to get a car so I can give your truck back. Even though I've learned to love the ugly beast."

"Are you calling my truck an ugly beast? She's beautiful."

"Beauty is in the eyes of the beholder." I rolled my eyes. "Don't forget I mentioned that I loved her."

"I love you," Jesse said and immediately looked mortified that came out of his mouth.

"What? No—you do?" I stammered. I felt heat flood to my cheeks, and my heart started thudding so loudly, it was roaring in my ears.

"Um, what if I said yes? I do? Is that weird?" he said, quietly, questioning.

"I don't know. I guess it depends on if I love you too." Shit. I didn't know what to say, and now I just backed myself into a corner and had to say something. So after a long silence I said the stupidest thing imaginable. "I'll have to think on that one."

I said it with a grin and then kissed him silly trying to put my emotions into the kiss rather than having to say it aloud. The truth was, I did love him. The words stuck there in my throat, begging to be let out, but my body wouldn't let me say them.

I pushed him back onto the sofa and straddled his hips. I placed my hands under his shirt into his hard chest. His skin was hot, and I felt my way up then down his taut stomach muscles until I reached the button of his jeans. Still unable to look at him after my fumbling statement, my lips followed the path my hand just took as my fingers worked his fly. When I unclasped all of the buttons, I reached in and wrapped my hands around his thick hard cock. I looked down at the swollen purple head and licked my lips. "Pull down those jeans babe, will you?" I asked, finally meeting his eyes. They were dark and filled with lust. He kept his eyes locked with mine as he pushed down his jeans enough to free all those glorious parts of him completely.

I leaned down and traced my tongue along the seam, licking down the hard, veiny shaft. It jerked in my hand in response. I licked up the other side in a long languorous stroke with my tongue, taking in his all male scent and warm heat. My mouth hovered above the tip and I let my eyes meet his as I took the velvet soft length of him into my mouth. It took a couple strokes with my hand and mouth before I nearly took him all the way, and I vowed I would work to take him fully one day soon. The only other person I had done this to easily fit, never reaching the back of my throat. But Jesse was huge, and while I should be intimidated, I was only determined to take as much of him inside me as I could.

When I felt him reach the back of my throat, I used my hand to cover the rest of him and started working him in and out, sucking as hard as I could.

"Rina, oh God, Rina, I can't—going to come." He gripped the back of my hair and tried to pull me up.

I bared down harder, pulling faster, taking more and more of him until instead of pulling me up, his fisted hand in my hair moved in rhythm with me. The slight pulling of my hair turned me on even more so, and I could feel my own panties flooding with wetness.

Jesse started moving frantically, and gave one last attempt to stop me, but I wouldn't let up. I felt his release pulse down my throat, the salty warm taste of him heating me to my core. As he filled me, I kept sucking and swallowing determined to get every last drop.

I didn't say anything. I didn't have to. The look in his eyes said it all and I sat up and smiled at him.

"Please believe me when I tell you this," Jesse said with a hooded satiated smile. "That was the single most amazing blow job I've ever had."

I'd never wanted to please somebody like that. Ever. I wanted to do that for him every night of my life if it meant I'd see that look on his face again. *I love you*, I thought to myself, wishing I could say it aloud.

28

Jesse

I fucking told her I loved her. What the hell was I thinking? It just came out, not of my own free will. And she didn't say it back. *Fuck.* I had to have scared her off. She threw herself into distracting me with that amazing mouth of hers. I have never in my life had a girl suck me off like that.

I loved her. I didn't mean to say it right then and there, but I did, and now the ball was in her court. That is, if she still wanted to see me. I had plans to see her later in the week, and she didn't seem awkward. I'm sure she didn't.

I left Rina's late afternoon and went right to my shop. I was working on a 1972 Chevrolet Nova SS Tribute that I wanted to bring to a big show over near Albany in October. It was nearly done. I was proud of her. My restorations were getting some local attention, and I was hoping to get a pretty price on this one. I was working underneath the chassis when Jameson strolled in.

"Hey, big brother, long time no see."

I rolled out from under the car and looked up at him. "Hey, asshole. Ready to get back to school?"

"I am. Can't wait to finish this shit, you know?"

"I do." I didn't go to college, but I did go through several mechanic certifications over the years. It was hard work. "Seeing the finish line is the best feeling in the world."

"It is, it is. I'm just not sure what to do next," he said leaning against the workstation nearest.

"You can figure it out then. For now, get that paper and be proud to be the first Singer to get a college degree." I was standing now in front of him and wiped some of the grime off my hands with the rag hanging from my waist. "I'm proud of you, you know."

I looked at him, and he looked back. We stood there all serious for a few beats before Jameson chucked, "Thanks Dad." We both huffed and looked away. Then Jameson said, "I mean it, Jesse. You are the only dad I've known and I'm glad it was you there for me and Mom."

"Well, you don't remember Dad, but I do. Anybody could've done a better job than that asshole."

"Like I said, I'm glad it was you. I know you gave up a lot to help us. Your own chance at college even. You stayed in this town to support Mom when she got hurt, and then me. I owe you the world."

"No, you don't. Look, I love my job and I love what I do. I have friends, family, and I get to make these badass cars. No complaints. You got me kid?"

"These cars are badass," he said, walking over to take a closer look at the Nova.

Steve just finished prepping her for paint. She was going to be a sleek and shiny deep-blood red. I couldn't wait to see her finished.

"Yup, they are," I said, admiring my work.

"So, Rina?" Jameson moved his eyes from the car over to me.

"What about her?"

"You and her like—" He wiggled his eyebrows.

"You're a dick." I swatted my towel at him, and he jumped out of the way.

"Seriously, bro. You've got to hang on to that one. She's a keeper. You're going to hang on to her, right?"

"With everything I can," I said and went back to work.

29

Jesse

Three days later, I helped Jameson load his bags into his truck, and followed him over to O'Dells where we were meeting for a farewell lunch. Steve and Michael were already waiting, apparently starting with a few drinks early. It was due. My boys had been covering for me a lot lately, and I cut them all loose late in the morning.

I split off on the drive over to pick up Rina. When I pulled up, she was on the porch waiting with Max. That dog never left her side without her saying so, but she must've whispered something when I turned in the drive, because he launched off the porch like a torpedo.

"Hey there, Max," I said as I hopped out of the truck and bent down to rough all along the length of his back as he circled around me. He hopped up against me with his body.

He wasn't a licker, thank God, but he did like to body slam and headbutt.

"Max, in the house," Rina called from the porch and the happy dog ran another lap around me before beelining straight for her.

"Sorry, boy, can't go to the bar," she said as she shut him inside.

She turned toward me, her perfect bow lips in an adorable little pout. "I hate to leave him home."

"I know you do, but we'll make it up to him," I said walking toward her. She was carrying a large box that I immediately took out of her hands. "Whoa, who are you feeding? An army?"

"Jameson can eat like an army. I have a few packages in there for the guys, and Annie too."

I bent down to give her a soft kiss on the mouth. "Mmmmm, I've missed you."

Her eyes lingered closed after the kiss. "I've missed you too. Can you please stay with me tonight?"

Not awkward, and I relaxed, knowing that I didn't scare her away with the "I love you" line.

"Absolutely. Without a doubt. I've missed those gorgeous lips too much to stay away." I kissed her long and full, and before we both got carried away, she escaped and hopped off the porch.

I watched her walk to the truck. Her curvy, yet slim figure hopped onto the step and into the cab. She was wearing tight-fitting jeans that fit every curve of her ass, her favorite cowboy boots, and a T-shirt that said "Rock 'n Roll" with a rolling pin on the front. She'd traded in her ponytail for two braids down the back, emphasizing her big brown eyes and freckles across her nose. She was adorable. I was done for.

I hopped in the cab next to her and she scooted close to me on the bench seat. I put my arm around her shoulders, backed out of the driveway and headed out to meet the boys.

"And then, Jesse, convinced the truck could handle it, drove straight up onto the boulder, and broke the axle. Took four hours to get the truck out, not to mention the damage." Jameson was animatedly telling the embarrassing story.

"Why'd you have to tell that story, you asshole?" I said ribbing my little brother.

"Because you, despite what others may think, are not perfect," Steve said, his trademark smile out in full force.

"I think he's perfect," Rina said wrapping her arms around me and kissing my cheek.

"Oh, Jesse, you're so perfect." Jameson snorted. "You're so wonderful." He puckered his lips and made squeaky kissing sounds. He wiggled his eyebrows, still making those sounds.

God, my brother could be so immature.

"Fuck off," Rina and I said in unison.

We were all seated around one of the tables away from the bar. The bar was brightly lit, as it was afternoon. Annie liked to let the light in for the afternoon lunch crowd, giving the bar an entirely different vibe during the day. Our burgers just arrived, and Steve snatched a french fry off Rina's plate.

"Hey! Those are mine. All mine!"

Rina playfully swatted at him as he bounced backward

out of the way. Michael, saying nothing as usual, took a swig from his beer bottle, silently observing the banter.

We ate and laughed and enjoyed each other's company. We were like a little family, each of us finally finding our place. But the elephant in the room, Jameson heading back to school, lingered over us all.

Finally, my brother got up and declared, "Well you fuckers, and lady, I've got to hit the road if I want to make it back at a decent hour."

The guys all stood and said their goodbyes, and Rina and I walked him out to his truck. I got the box Rina made for him and said, "This is a care package from Rina."

Jameson took the box from me. "You better have plans to marry that girl when I get back."

I smiled and patted him on the back. Rina blushed at the remark as Jameson set the box in his truck and turned back to her.

"You, you beautiful woman. Take care of my brother. He needs help, even with the simple things. Like getting the mail or paying bills. I don't know how he made it this far in life."

Rina laughed and gave him a big hug. "Don't worry, I've got him. I'll be sending you more care packages, so don't hoard!" she scolded.

Jameson hopped in the truck and leaned his head out the window. "See. Marry her. I need a sister." He winked, turned over the engine, put the truck in gear, and headed down the road.

I grabbed the last of Rina's bakery bags out of my truck, and we held hands back to the bar and didn't say anything, both feeling the sadness of saying goodbye, even if it was only for a few months.

I brought my bag over to the boys while Rina went to the bar to see Annie. When I looked over at her, I saw her handing Annie the bag. Annie took a peek inside and her eyes lit up. I saw the girls engage in friendly chatter and turned back to the table.

I put the bag in the middle of the table and said, "I don't know why she likes you fuckers, but Rina baked you some cookies."

"Oh yeah," Steve said, and all three rose from their seats and dug into the bag like starving men.

"I love these chocolate coconut cookies! Yes!" Steve said as he practically shoved the entire thing in his mouth.

Michael reached in and grabbed one too and merely said, "Good," but a grin edged the corners of his mouth as he took a bite.

I watched them sit down reveling in Rina's cookies when I looked around to find the woman herself. Rina didn't look happy anymore. She was standing, facing the other end of the bar, arms across her chest. I could see in her posture she was wound tight and on the defensive.

I followed the direction of her anger and saw Mandy sitting at the end of the bar. Some guy had his arm around her waist, but she was clearly saying something across the bar to Rina. I couldn't hear her, but I heard Annie say, "Get out of my bar Mandy, before you regret it."

I made my way swiftly over to Rina's side and asked, "What did she say to you?" Then I turned to Mandy. "What did you say to her, Mandy?"

Mandy had the gall to smile at me and wave? Like to say hello? Like she wasn't just being nasty at all. Weird. Creepy and weird.

"Nothing," Rina said as she turned me toward her so we were chest to chest. She reached up and wrapped her arms around my neck and standing on her tiptoes she whispered in my ear, "Kiss me, stupid."

I didn't argue. I kissed the woman. Hard, lots of tongue, and I let my hands roam all over her body. When I broke the kiss, she looked at me and winked. She then turned to Mandy, "How about that, bitch? He's mine."

Wow. My girl was harsh. I liked it.

"You fucking cunt. He'll be back. There is no way he'd give up this," indicating her body, "for your ugly, pathetic ass."

"No, Mandy," I said. "Never gonna happen. Get out of here. Go home, or go fuck that guy in your car, or whatever it is you're doing these days." I didn't normally talk to women like that, but she pissed me the hell off.

I had no idea what she was doing at the bar in the middle of the day. She wasn't a lush or anything, and I hadn't known her to be a daylight barfly. If I had to take a guess, the poor sucker next to her had something she wanted, and she was working some angle to get it.

"Get out, Mandy. Now. Before I force you out," Annie said. Nobody fucked with Annie. Not even a troublemaker like Mandy. People around town knew better.

Mandy grabbed the guy by the hand and dragged him out the door. What did it say about him that he didn't even protest? Mandy was beautiful, and an easy piece of ass, apparently. I'm guessing the guy didn't give a shit what she wanted, as long as he got to fuck her too.

"You okay, baby?" I said looking down, stroking the ends of her braids.

"Just shook up, is all. I'll be fine."

"I liked how you went all cavewoman on me. I'm so turned on now, I'd like to take you out to the truck." I nuzzled into her neck. She was warm and her cheeks were flushed. She leaned in to me and then pushed me off gently.

"I'm good."

"What did she say to you?"

"Nothing."

"Rina?"

"It's nothing, Jesse. I'm not going to let her get to me, alright?"

She leaned in close to me so nobody else could hear. "But I think something's going on with her. I mean, I don't know her at all, never even talked to her before. But I'm telling you there's something not right there."

"I think she's gotten worse. Honest, she wasn't like this until the baby thing and we broke up. She was always needy and bitchy to other women, but I used to think it was insecurities. Thinking she had a bum lot in life. But I know better now that it's what you do with your lot that counts."

"Let's just get back to the guys and have a good time, mmm?" Rina said, sticking her hand in my back jean pocket and steering me to the table. I bent down and kissed the top of her head. She turned over her shoulder to the pretty bartender. "Thanks Annie, I owe you one."

"No problem, hon. That bitch had it coming. Keep bringing me cookies and I'll kick out anybody you want."

30

Rina

The rest of the afternoon went without incident. I was still reeling from the Mandy thing. What a crackpot. While talking to Annie, Mandy sidled up to me at the bar and said, "So, I see Jesse really lowered his standards this time. You just wait, he'll come back to me. He needs to. He can't get enough, just like last night."

Now, I know Jesse wasn't with her last night. I mean I didn't have proof he wasn't, because he wasn't with me, but I knew deep down inside he wouldn't go near her. That girl had something crazy going all up in her mind. I could see it in her eyes, and in her appearance. Her hair was just a little too messy, her lipstick a little too smeared, and her dress was a little too wrinkled. And why did she wear a clubbing dress to the bar in the afternoon? It was like she never went home last night. Something about the whole thing rubbed me wrong, and not just because she was Jesse's ex.

It was early evening when we left O'Dell's to head home. It was tough saying goodbye to Jameson. I really like that kid. He filled the little brother role in my life, and I was looking forward to seeing him again at Christmas. *Whoa.* Did that mean I was planning long term with Jesse? It hit me that I was looking at a future. A real future, with a house, a dog, and a man. Wow. I don't know why that caught me off guard, but it did. I was staying with Jesse because I couldn't imagine not being with him. His family felt like my family.

Jesse pulled us into my driveway. We walked to the porch and as soon as I opened the door, fifty pounds of Max ran out. He circled us a few times in his happy dog glee, then ran to the yard to take care of some business. When I stepped into the doorway Jesse stopped.

"Shit. Babe, I'm sorry. I have to turn off the booth heater for that old Nova Steve just painted. I've got to go back to the shop and take care of it. I won't be long, I promise."

"No problem. I'd like to take a shower and change anyway. I'll make us some popcorn and we'll settle in for a movie?"

"Perfect," Jesse said as he turned back to his truck.

Max ran onto the porch again and was nudging my hand with his head. "Hey, take Max with you? He's been in the house for hours. You know he loves a car ride."

"Absolutely! Be back soon." He gave me a quick kiss. "Come on, Max!" he yelled as he walked down the path.

Max leaped off the steps in a single bound. I watched him open the door and Max jumped inside. He took a couple excited turns and then gleefully stuck his head out the window to enjoy the car ride. I smiled to myself at the goofy dog and went into the house.

I was longing for a bath all day. I'd been unusually tired the last few days with the remodel on Main Street and I'd been longing for a deep hot soak. I turned on the water to fill the tub and added some of my favorite bath salts. As the water ran, creating a steam-filled corner of paradise, I headed down the hall to change, and find my bathrobe.

I remembered my robe was in the dryer and headed downstairs to the laundry. When I walked by the front door, I noticed it ajar. That was weird, I always shut it when home alone. I walked over and pulled it shut. I made it to the laundry and opened the dryer door to get my bathrobe.

Pain exploded in the back of my head. I stumbled down to one knee, stunned. What was happening?

Another pain erupted through my skull as it registered. I was hit on the back of the head and fell to the floor. I didn't pass out though. I rolled over on my back, in a daze trying to figure out what happened. When I looked up, I saw Mandy standing over me with one of Grandpa's large metal horse head bookends.

The last thing I heard was, "I got to get rid of you, bitch," before her arms swung down and the world went black.

31

Rina

I came awake in the dark. My head hurt and I could feel sticky and tacky liquid on my face and hair. Blood. I was bleeding from my head. *Calm down,* I told myself, head wounds always bleed like the dickens. I could feel rivulets of it rolling down my temple and the side of my face. My ears were ringing and felt clogged. More blood dripped into my ear. I turned my head to get some of the liquid out. I tried to open my eyes, but only the left one opened, the right was swollen shut. Not a lot of good it did though. I couldn't see anything.

I tried to move my hands and feet, but they were both bound, my hands behind my back. Oh, I hurt. Every breath hurt. Ribs? Do I have broken ribs? What happened to me? Then I remembered. Mandy.

She was in my house. She hit me and knocked me out.

Did she beat me when I was unconscious? My ribs were by far the most painful. I could only take short shallow breaths. I started to panic. *Stay calm, Rina,* I tried to tell myself as I focused on breathing and figure out what was happening.

I was moving. It was dark. I was tied up. It dawned on me that I was in the trunk of a car. This wasn't helping me panic less. Where was I going and why couldn't I breathe? *You have had a worse beating than this, Rina. Suck it up. Think!* Right, I had to stay calm and think.

I tried to count how long we were driving. I didn't notice any turns, so I think we were on a single road for about ten minutes. We were also going uphill. Of course, I was unconscious for part of the ride. This information didn't really help me, but it helped me concentrate on something other than the burning pain in my chest.

We slowed down and turned onto gravel. A few beats later, we stopped. Parking lot? The car engine shut off, and I heard steps crunching on gravel. The trunk opened, and I tried to look up at the looming figure over me. A flashlight shined too brightly in my face and I squinted at the sudden intrusion.

I could see the outline of Mandy. She was still in her skin tight club dress. Her hair was sticking up all over. She bent over with a large knife and cut my bound feet loose.

"Get out," she demanded, cold and detached. I struggled to move and failed. Surprisingly strong hands grabbed me by the duct tape binding my hands, pulling me to a seated position. I screamed at the pain but wouldn't let myself fall back down.

"I said, get the fuck out," she repeated, and this time when

I struggled, she grabbed me by the hair and dragged my torso over the back of the trunk.

I scrambled my legs and feet over the edge to keep from falling, but the pain in my ribs was too much and I fell over hard, onto the gravel lot. I wheezed and coughed, still struggling to get my legs underneath me. Eventually I stood up but hunched over. My shirt was wet and cool against me. That head wound must be bigger than I thought. *Shit.* I started to feel dizzy.

"You can't die here. I got to take you in and hide you. It was hard enough getting you into the trunk. You're going to have to walk."

Again, she was so calm and detached. As if the entire situation wasn't scary enough, her cold, dead eyes were horrifying.

She brandished the flashlight again, along with a huge hunting knife, and pointed them both to a trail into the woods. I looked around trying to get my bearings. I knew where I was. What were the chances she would bring me here? To my old hiking spot with Grandpa. And why here where I first met Jesse? My mind went fuzzy again, and I looked down at my ribs. There was an awful lot of blood there.

I looked up at Mandy in horror. "What? What did you do to me?"

"Oh, that. That's just going to make my life harder, damn it. I forgot about the stupid bucket of tools Jesse left in my trunk a while back. I dropped you on it while getting your ugly ass in the trunk. I think something stabbed you somewhere, maybe a screwdriver, I dunno. I did manage to get it out from under you though," she said matter-of-fact.

She stared at my rib area where the blood was pooling, then let out a deep bored breath. "Well, let's get you walking, as far as we can anyway." And again, waved her flashlight and knife indicating the trail into the forest.

What. The. Fuck? She'd gone wacko. That was the only word for it. Insane, cray-cray, loony. Bat shit crazy. There was no way I was going to go into those woods. Everybody knows to not let your attacker take you anywhere. You will never be seen again. You're better off taking the bullet in the parking lot, right?

"Why are we here?" I wanted to keep her talking, and it might be my only chance. Something broke inside this woman and it was terrifying. I looked at her, really looked at her.

She was in a skin tight red mini dress and black stiletto heels. It was obvious she hadn't thought this through, just in her clothing choices alone. Her blonde tresses were sticking up in a million directions as if she were pulling at it with her hands. Her mascara was running down her face, and she looked at me like I was a cockroach she needed to stamp out. I used to think she was beautiful, but now all I saw was ugliness. She stopped and faced me head on. I kept my eye on the knife, ready to dodge it if needed.

"I was going to get him back, you know. I had it all planned out. He was going to rescue me from an abusive new boyfriend. You know, one that would leave bruises. He can't resist that shit."

I stared at her in shock, trying to drum up a response to keep her talking. "But why are we here?"

She started pacing back and forth in front of me and then scanned the lot. "I was here you know, the day you met Jesse. Right over there." She pointed to an area to my left.

"I was in the back of Timmy Weston's van. Boy, that guy is a disgusting slob, you know? He smells like mushrooms," she said in remembrance. "You know he still lives with his parents? Forty years old and we had to drive up here to get it on? Pathetic."

I remembered that van. It was the only other vehicle in the lot that day besides Jesse's and my vehicles. I thought it was empty.

"So you were here with Timmy, and did he hurt you?" I needed to keep her talking and distracted.

"Hurt me? Fuck no. The guy couldn't even get hard no matter how long I tried to work him." She looked at me like I was stupid and then continued to chatter. "But he paid me good whether he got off or not."

"You were fucking guys for money?"

"Because of Jesse!" she boomed. "He broke up with me. I needed things, and I needed money."

"How about a job?" I couldn't stop myself from being a smart-ass.

Her enraged eyes locked on mine and she slapped me across the face. I wobbled and landed on one knee trying desperately not to lose consciousness. It was really getting hard to breathe, and I barely had the strength to stand back up.

"A job! Why should I bust my ass forty hours a week when I look like this? Girls that look like me are supposed to have it easy. Isn't that right? Girls that look like *you* are the ones that are supposed to work. I was Miss Teen Pennsylvania, you know. That was supposed to be my ticket. I was supposed to be taken care of."

She was crazy. Did I say that yet? I had to find a way out of here and soon. My vision was getting fuzzy and the edges dark. I was going to pass out. Probably die.

"Anyway, Timmy and I were in the back of his van. I was trying to suck his limp ass dick to life, when we heard the commotion with the bear. We thought that shit was pretty funny. That thing crawled into your window and couldn't get itself out. It was crying and screaming and making a general mess of things. I saw you walking out of the woods, face bruised and generally looking like hell. Then Jesse was there.

"What are the chances? That he and I end up in the same place at the same time? I knew we were meant to be again. But then he saw you. You and your bruises. You who needed to be rescued with a ride home. You, who were not even pretty, but I saw. I saw how he looked at you."

"Mandy, I—"

"HE LET YOU DRIVE HIS TRUCK!" She screamed so loud at me I stumbled backward.

I was really unsteady now. My wrists were tied so tight I couldn't feel my hands. I leaned forward to steady myself.

"He never lets anybody drive his truck. We were together for over a year and he never let me drive his truck."

"I'm sorry, Mandy. I didn't know." What else could I say? I read once that if you were kidnapped that you should sympathize with your kidnapper, try to appear human. I didn't know if it would work, but every moment I didn't have to walk into the woods with Mandy and her big ass knife gave me time to think of a way out of this.

"I never saw him before that day. He helped me out of a

bad situation. You know what kind of guy he is. You shouldn't blame him for it."

Mandy was pacing back and forth, pulling at her hair and waving the knife. It was like she didn't hear me at all.

"And then he started hanging out with you, and taking care of YOU, when it should've been me. I was the one that needed him." She started sobbing.

Fuck me being nice. It wasn't working, I was running out of time, and this was starting to piss me the hell off. "You know what? You're pathetic, and I'm not listening to your dumb ass crybaby shit anymore. Take care of yourself for once. No wonder Jesse hates you. You're a taker Mandy and a user. Bite me. I don't want to hear your shit anymore."

Probably not the best thing to do when bleeding from the chest, with a head wound and your arms tied behind your back. But I could feel darkness closing in around my vision. I really was running out of time, so I kept going. "What have you ever given him other than try to trap him? I know all about you, *Mandy*. I know how you told him you were having his baby. How you purposely got pregnant by another man. How Jesse found out and dumped you for it. And when you lost the baby? You had nothing!" I screamed back at her.

Mandy stopped moving and stood stock still like a deer in headlights. I could see her hands trembling at her sides, her face contorted in utter madness before she screamed, "I'm going to kill you!" and ran straight at me.

32

Jesse

Max and I drove down to my shop, and I took care of the Nova rather quickly. I stopped for a moment and admired the killer paint job Steve had pulled off. Dark red was definitely the right color for this one. She was gorgeous.

On the way back I thought of Rina and how far we had come in our relationship. I chuckled to myself thinking of how she handled Mandy tonight. She hadn't told me she loved me, but I knew she did. She was just scared. She was possessive and confident in us, and that really turned me on. I didn't realize how much I needed a girl like Rina until, well, Rina.

I worked really hard to get where I was. I also sacrificed a lot. Jameson was right. I gave up my chance for school to take care of him and Mom. But I had done something with myself. I worked my ass off at the garage, and I loved what I did.

Okay, old ladies and oil changes, not so much, but my restoration projects? Taking a piece of the broken past and making it whole again was what I truly loved.

Rina worked her ass off too. She lost part of herself, but through her determination and grit she'd come a long way. She could do anything she put her mind to, and that made her even more beautiful than anything you could see on the surface.

I was thinking of all of those things when I pulled back into Rina's drive. Max immediately jumped out of the car and started sniffing around the yard. Thinking he had business to take care of, as dogs always seem to have to do, I walked up to the porch and noticed the screen was shut, but the main door was open.

"Hey, Rina, we're back," I said as Max tore past me when I opened the screen door. No answer. I heard water running upstairs and realized she was still in the bath. I walked up the stairs smiling, Max tore down the stairs past me. "Silly dog," I muttered.

I could hear Max's nails clacking throughout the house on the hardwood floors as I made my way to the bathroom door when I heard a splashing sound from below. I looked down and saw my foot in a puddle of water. I tracked the water to the bathroom door, and it was everywhere. "Rina? Are you okay?" I asked loudly and rushed toward the door.

There was nobody in the small bathroom and water was running up and over the tub. The loud running of the water suppressed my hearing, and I reached over and turned off the faucet. The room went silent except for the water sloshing onto the floor. I could still hear Max clacking around the house. He was moving fast from room to room. Other than that, it was too quiet, and I knew nobody was home. My heart started pounding and blood rushed to my ears.

"Rina!" I hollered as I ran into the bedroom. Nothing looked out of place or disturbed, but Rina wasn't there. I ran down the stairs into the living room and then the kitchen. Max circled around me and started whining and then barking in a low tone.

"Max? Where's Rina?" Max took off down the hall toward the laundry, and I followed.

Max stood in the middle of the laundry room. The dryer door was ajar and Rina's bathrobe was hanging halfway out of the opening. I scanned the floor, and I saw it. Blood. Not a lot, but enough to throw me into a panic.

"Max, out of the room." I pointed, and Max went and stood outside the hall. I took in the tiny room. I could see blood was smudged, like it had been wiped up, or dragged over. I followed the smear out into the hall and found several droplets of red. Oh shit. Fear engulfed me and my heart was now pounding furiously. I forced myself to move slowly and try to figure this out. The small trail, a drop every few feet, led me onto the porch to gaze out into the yard. Max, once again, bolted past.

"Rina!" I called out into the yard. Nothing. Max was pawing at the ground and I ran over. Tire tracks in the grass led up to the porch. What the hell? I scanned the yard and noticed a bucket on the ground with what looked like tools scattered about. They looked familiar, and it took me a few breaths to place them. Mandy had several rotted boards on her porch that I went over to replace a while back. It was a small job, so I threw a few tools in a bucket. How did they get here? I had no idea, but I wasn't going to waste time figuring that out. Rina was missing, there was blood in her house, and it looked like Mandy had something to do with it.

I knew something was off about Mandy lately, but I never thought she was actually dangerous. "Shit! Shit! Shit!" I fumbled my phone from my pocket and dialed 911.

"Nine-one-one operator, what is your emergency?"

"I'm Jesse Singer. I believe my girlfriend has been injured and taken. She is not in her home. I found it unlocked and signs of struggle."

After answering a few more questions and giving the address, the dispatcher announced, "Please stay on the line, I am dispatching an officer to that address."

I waited for what seemed like forever. "Sir, I have officers en route, they are five minutes out," said a very calm and monotone voice.

"I think she was taken by Mandy Garvey. Her address is 8431 Pine Hollow Drive Can you send a car to that address?"

"Sir, officers will arrive shortly. Please stay on the line."

"I need to look for her," I said into the phone, not really talking to the dispatcher, but to myself. Where the heck would she take her? I hadn't a clue. Max was still circling the yard, whining and yelping.

"Max, where's Rina?" Max's ears perked up at my voice and he ran toward me, circling me.

"Max, find Rina," I said. He sniffed at the air and took off down the drive. "Max!" I called.

"I think her dog is tracking her. I'm going to chase the dog," I said to the woman on the line.

"Sir, please wait for an officer."

I hung up the phone and ran to my truck.

I peeled out of the driveway, now in search of Max. Now,

there was a part of me that realized this was borderline crazy. This wasn't a television show, and Max sure as fuck wasn't Lassie. I was desperate and grasping at anything at all to keep me moving forward. *Find Rina, find Rina,* wouldn't stop looping through my brain.

I spotted the dog running down the middle of the street. I slowed down when I neared and leaned out the window.

"Max!" But the dog just kept going. He slowed to a jog when we rounded a bend, sniffed along the curb, then took off into a sprint up the road.

I saw on a documentary once that search and rescue dogs can track cars in grass and on curbs. But Max was not an SAR dog, and I knew next to nothing about it anyway. We got about two miles down the road, Max periodically stopping, and me trying not to lose my shit. I was convinced I was losing my mind. I picked up my phone again and called Steve.

"Hey, dickhead," Steve answered in his usual playful voice.

"Steve, Rina's missing. I think Mandy took her. I called the police, but I left. I need you to go to Rina's house and meet them there," I blurted out.

"Dude, *what*?" Steve practically shouted.

"Go to Rina's house. Cops are on their way."

"Sure, man, sure. Where are you?"

"I'm following the dog down the street. I don't know what else to do. I know it sounds crazy, but I've got nothing else."

"What happened?"

"There's blood in her house and I'm not going to get into the details but looks like she was taken by car somewhere. Max is with me. Actually, Max took off down the road. I didn't know what to do but follow the damn dog. Fuck!" I pounded the steering wheel.

"Ok, I'm on my way. Look, animals can do the darndest things. Stick with the dog. I'm calling Michael, he's closer."

"Okay, Okay. I'll do that. Call me when you get there."

"Will do. And Jesse, we'll get her back." And he hung up.

Just as I disconnected with Steve, Max stopped. We were at a crossroads. He sniffed the air, then the ground. He started doing his circle thing. I pulled over and got out of the truck. I walked into the middle of the road with him. With a sinking feeling, I knew whatever he was chasing, he lost it. He ran to me and nudged my hand with his head. I bent down to hug him. "It's okay, Max, we'll find her."

We stood there in the middle of the road, in the dark. Town was to the left, and to the right was up to Parson's Lake, where I first met Rina. Max was breathing heavy from running. He let out a whine with each labored breath. I kept stroking his fur to calm him, and if I was honest with myself, it calmed me too. I could hear sirens in the other direction, I'm assuming on their way to Rina's house.

My phone rang again. "Mikey," I answered.

"I'm pulling in now," Michael said on the other line. "Steve is still ten minutes out. Wait. I see Lou Ortega. I'll talk to him."

He hung up. Great. Michael barely spoke to anybody, but I knew I could count on him to shed that hostile exterior and get the facts. That's what Michael did, he could assess and solve problems better than anybody I knew.

I was now pacing up and down the length of the truck when Michael called back. "Lou says they sent a car to Mandy's house. No news."

He hung up again. What the fuck?

I had to make a decision. I couldn't stay here on the side of an empty road any longer. My mind raced with places I might find Mandy, but there was none. Her home, The Diner, and O'Dells. O'Dells was out. It was a public place, not to mention Annie was there. It'd be suicidal to go there. The Diner was full of people too. If she wasn't at her house, then—

"Fuck!" I yelled to no one. Max let out a long whine as if saying the same.

I saw headlights coming down the road from further up the hill. They were far off but grew brighter as the car ranged in closer. The car was zigzagging across the line. It wasn't going fast. It was drifting down the hill without any acceleration. It swerved to the left then jerked quickly to the right. It didn't correct itself. Instead, it rolled slowly down a shallow embankment and stopped when it smashed into a large pine tree.

"Oh shit." The car was far enough away that I couldn't identify it, but my stomach dropped to the floor *because I knew*. I knew without a doubt it was Rina.

"Max, in the truck." He didn't hesitate, and we raced up to the wrecked car. When we got closer, I saw it was Mandy's piece of shit Taurus, and inside I saw a head of dark hair.

"Rina!" I threw the truck in park while still in motion. It jerked violently to a stop while I jumped out running toward the car, Max quickly passing me. Max was whining and barking, paws up in the driver's side window when I arrived. I pulled open the door and saw Rina slumped over the steering wheel.

"Oh God, Rina. Baby," I said as I gently leaned her back

against the seat. She was bleeding from her head and looked as pale as death. Her lips were chalky, and blood matted her hair everywhere. One eye was puffy and swollen shut. My blood ran cold at the sight of her.

She slowly turned her head toward me, "Jesse?" she said so softly I barely heard her.

"I've got you, baby. It's going to be okay. Stay still, I got you." I stroked her hair while Max struggled to get into the car. "Max, down," I said gently, and thank goodness he listened. He muscled his way between us and rested his head on her knee. I stroked her hair and her face as I picked up my phone and called Michael.

"Yeah?"

"She's here! I have her. Mikey, she's hurt real bad. Send an ambulance. I'm near the crossroads of Parsons and Cape." This time I hung up, trusting my friend would make the call.

"Jesse? I'm so sorry," Rina said. This time her breathing was labored. It took three breaths to get those words out.

"Shhhhh, Rina. Don't talk. Help is coming, you're going to be alright. I promise. Plus, what do you have to be sorry for anyway? Huh?"

"I didn't say I love you back," she slurred. Her one good eye flitted open for a second and looked directly at me. "I love you too." It came out in the smallest whisper. Her eyes closed again.

"You're going to be fine, baby. I'm going to hear you say that to me every day for the rest of my life. Do you hear me? Rina, I love you so much. I don't know how you got here and why you're in this car, but I'm so proud of you. You are so strong and brave."

Tears were rolling down my cheeks now as I stroked her

softly and kept talking. She wasn't responding anymore, but I could see she was still breathing.

I could hear the ambulance for a while now and it seemed to take forever for them to arrive. They quickly took command, and I had to let Rina go and let the paramedics do their job. Steve pulled up behind the ambulance as they were loading her in. Max tried to follow, of course.

"Max, no," I said. He backed off.

"We have to get her to the hospital fast. Besides the head trauma, she has suffered multiple stab wounds, and could have internal injuries. She's lost a lot of blood. Are you coming?"

I looked around at Max, at my truck. Steve piped in, "Go, I got all this. We'll meet you at the hospital."

I gave my friend a nod and jumped into the ambulance.

33

Jesse

They took Rina straight into surgery when we arrived at the hospital. After all of the chaos of the last couple hours, I was suddenly alone. I sat in the waiting room, and well, waited. Soon, Steve and Michael came through the front doors.

"Any news?" Steve asked.

"Not yet, she's still in surgery."

"I know some of these guys, she's in good hands," Steve replied.

"It was scary in the ambulance, man. They kept trying to give her an IV, but she had lost so much blood. There was so much going on, I couldn't understand, but they got her stabilized. They located two stab wounds, one was really deep, and they couldn't assess the damage."

"It's going to be okay." Steve pulled his hands through his

thick black hair. "She's going to be okay." This he said to himself and spun around to pace the room.

Michael gave me a squeeze on the shoulder and a nod, then went to sit on one of the hard plastic chairs. Legs spread out, arms over chest, mean face on. Hell, *I* was scared to go near him.

"What if she isn't? What if she isn't?" I said throwing my arms in the air. "I love her, man," I said when Steve paced back in my direction.

"I know you do, brother. We all do. Have a seat and wait with us. It's all we can do at this point."

"Where's Max?"

"I dropped him off with Annie. Rina's house is a crime scene. She was happy to take him."

The double emergency room doors slid open and Betsy and June came rushing in.

"Oh my God. What happened?" Betsy rushed out speaking to the entire room. I updated them on what I could. Betsy grasped June's hand tightly as they listened, horrified.

"Come on, Betsy." June led them to a row of empty chairs and waited with us.

Thirty agonizing minutes later, officer Lou Ortega followed two paramedics pushing a gurney carrying an awake and screaming Mandy. I couldn't understand what she was saying, but she was in pain. Her dress was torn and filthy, her hair standing up in a dozen directions, makeup oozing leaving black streaks down her face. She had a large bandage wrapped around her head, and her right ankle was propped up and in some sort of stabilizer. It was grotesquely swollen, and not at the right angle. If Jameson were here, he would've lost his lunch. *Shit,* Jameson. I had to call him as soon as I knew more.

I saw red. It took all I had not to go after that gurney. I think Steve and Michael saw me ready to blow and moved to block my view.

"I'm going to kill her. If Rina doesn't pull through this, I'm going to fucking kill her." They went through a set of double doors and I sat back down and put my head in my hands.

Lou came back a few minutes later. It wasn't the surgeon, but it was something. We all jumped to our feet. June ran over and gave her husband a hug.

Lou was five feet ten, with a stocky build. Clean shaven with a military style haircut, we'd had several friendly meetings over the years considering I had the town tow truck, and he was often the guy calling for one after an accident. He was even tempered, and an all-around good guy. He'd let you off with a warning more often than not, but he didn't give breaks to anybody causing a real danger. I respected that.

With his arm around his wife's waist, he said to me, "Jesse, I'll need a statement. You too Steve. Michael?"

We all nodded in agreement.

"What the hell happened?" I couldn't control myself any longer. I still had no idea how Rina got where she was and what happened to her. Other than she was seriously hurt, I didn't know anything else.

Lou took a deep breath; he looked tired. "Seems like Ms. Garvey went to Rina's, knocked her over the head and dragged her into the trunk of her car. She drove her up to the Parsons Lake trailhead intending to kill Rina somewhere in the woods."

"Holy fuck," Steve blew out.

"Ms. Garvey seems to think that Jesse belongs to her, and that Rina had taken him away from her, and needed to be eliminated."

"Eliminated?" This from June and Lou pulled his wife into him closer.

"Oh my God!" gasped Betsy.

"Apparently, Rina wouldn't cooperate with the plan and they fought in the parking lot. Somehow, Rina got away with Garvey's car. That's when you found her. We found Garvey injured in the parking lot screaming for help. I don't have any further details at this time."

Lou had his cop face on and was trying to be as emotionally unattached as possible. But we're a small town, with almost no crime. I could see he was shaken up.

We all stood silent for a while taking all of that in. I had already guessed most of that, being I was the one that discovered her missing, but still, it was hard to hear.

A tall thin woman wearing scrubs walked into the waiting area. Judging by the light lines around her eyes and mouth, I'm guessing she was in her early fifties. She had a warm smile and warmer dark brown eyes. "Family of Rina Sullivan," she called.

We all turned around at once and crowded toward her. "Here," I said. "We're her family."

The woman focused her words on me. I must've given off that desperate energy she sensed she needed to subdue. "Hello. I'm Dr. Leslie Draden. I performed surgery on Ms. Sullivan this evening. Ms. Sullivan made it through surgery, and we are expecting a full recovery."

I let out a huge breath, and I looked to the sky willing the tears to go back in.

"However," the doctor continued, "she's lost a lot of blood, and suffered two rather serious injuries. No major organs were damaged, but she does have two crushed ribs and a concussion that will take considerable time to heal."

"When can I, I mean we, see her?" I asked.

"She'll be moved from recovery shortly. I'll have a nurse find you when she is settled into her room."

"Thank you, Dr. Draden. Thank you," I said.

Suddenly, I was exhausted. I sat back into the chair, put my head in my hands and cried. I didn't care who saw.

34

Rina

Being stabbed twice was no picnic. My worst injury by far was the ribs and stabbing from the toolbox, i.e. stabbing number one. Jesse still found some absurd demented guilt about that, because they were his tools. I told him he was being ridiculous; he didn't pick me up and throw me in a trunk. I still don't know how Mandy did it. I told him to let it go. He did save my life after all. If not for him and Max finding me like he did, I probably wouldn't be here.

He wouldn't take any credit for that either. He said it was all Max. My dog was a hero. I agree with that too.

Max was a hero, and the best damn dog in the world. The local paper even called to write a story on him. While I really wanted to give my boy local celebrity status, I politely declined. I didn't want any of us being known for the terrible event we went through. Even Mandy. There is something very wrong with her. Something broke inside after the baby, and I sincerely hope she gets some help. Behind bars, of course. She still belongs there, but whatever her demons, they don't need to be shared with the world.

Jesse was right on one account, I totally kicked Mandy's ass. I almost died, mind you, but still I'm taking the win. Mandy ran at me with that knife, I ran straight at her, head down like a bull. After all, my hands were tied behind my back, so I didn't have many options. It hurt like hell, but I managed to knock her to the ground. She was wearing those stupid stiletto heels in a gravel parking lot. When she went down, she nearly twisted her ankle one hundred eighty degrees. I didn't realize it at the time, but the knife went into my left side about four inches, but fell free from her grip when we impacted. She screamed like nothing I ever heard. I don't blame her, ankle twisted as it was. I managed to get the knife behind me and cut myself free, then got into the car and drove down the hill. I barely remember the rest.

For all intents and purposes, Jesse had moved into my house these last three weeks. I insisted we put up Halloween decorations in the yard. Grandpa and I had done so all those years ago, and I wanted to revive the tradition.

I walked out onto the porch with two steaming cups of hot apple cider. Max was out in the front yard with Jesse, the latter staking in foam headstones near the front. Jesse was wearing a red and black flannel shirt, the same one he wore the first time I saw him. He was a welcome, beautiful sight, and when he turned and saw me, his mouth stretched wide in a grin. I swooned, as usual.

He bounded up the porch steps. "Hey there, beautiful."

He leaned down to give me a soft sensual kiss. He smelled

of woodsmoke and chilled air, and I leaned in closer so I could fill more of my senses.

"Hey there," I said back. "I brought something hot to drink, to help take the chill off."

He took one of the two mugs I was holding and cupped it in his hands. "I can think of something else that'll warm us up." He winked over his mug.

"Well, come on inside then," I purred back, my hands stroking his chest as I leaned into him.

"Oh, no, no, no, baby girl. Doc says to take it easy for one more week."

He started backing away from me. I stuck my lower lip out and frowned.

This was our daily conversation the last few days, and I kept losing. Jesse was scared of hurting me and was waiting for the all clear from the doctor. I insisted I was fine and kept pushing. I walked back to him and he backed near the top step. I traced up and down his chest with my palm. "Please, I'm fine. Come on in and play with me, or I'm going to be forced to play with myself."

He groaned as I turned around and walked inside.

I headed up to my room and laid down on my bed, back against the headboard and arms resting comfortably above my head. It only took a few minutes, but soon Jesse's big strong form filled the doorway. He gripped the jam tight, head hanging low, lust-filled eyes peering at mine.

"Woman, you're going to kill me."

"I love you," was all it took.

He pounced.

35

Six Months Later
Rina

It was the most beautiful day of the year and spring was a promise in the air. It was the first real day Betsy and I could set up the outdoor furniture for our shops. Business was fantastic. Eleanor Rose's name lived on through catered birthdays, special events, and daily in the bakery, accompanied with a fine cup of Betsy's Coffee, of course. We were both growing by leaps and bounds, and Betsy was now setting up an online store for us. Go figure Betsy would make us money selling mugs and T-shirts on the Internet.

I was busy wiping off tables while Betsy filled vases with fresh-cut flowers. The sun was shining, the birds were singing, and it was a good day to smile.

"When is Jesse stopping by?" Betsy asked.

"Should be any minute. He said he was putting the finishing touches on his latest project, then he'd be over."

"Hmmm," Betsy said with a grin.

"What?" I asked, now suspicious.

"Oh, nothing at all, hon. Help me out with these last vases, huh?"

After all the outside work was done, Betsy said, "Let's put up our feet for a few and watch the view."

And so we did. Main Street had brightened up over the winter and this spring. A few shop owners had followed our lead to give the town a fresh coat of paint, so to speak. Traffic had been increasing, and Song was now a popular tourist stop since the broken down tour bus incident. I guess bus drivers talk, who knew?

It reminded me of those quaint little towns of Americana you see on postcards and advertisements. People were meandering from shop to shop, and both Eleanor Rose, and Betsy's Coffee were starting to form lines at the counters. We each had enough business now to hire more staff for cashier work, and the new girls were behind the counter working hard. I was just about to go inside to help out with the growing crowd, when Betsy's phone pinged and I caught her glancing slyly at her screen, then texted furiously before stuffing it back into her pocket.

She looked over at me watching her and said, "Your man's almost here. Follow me."

She stood up and walked to the curb. She took out her phone and thumbed another quick text, and before I knew it, June came hustling down the sidewalk.

"I'm not missing this!" she practically screamed when she neared us.

"Missing what?" My eyes scanned from Betsy to June. "What the hell is going on?"

I looked back to Betsy. "Were you just texting my boyfriend?"

They both just stared at me wide eyed, clearly not knowing how to answer.

"Just want to see Jesse's new project is all," Betsy finally said, pretending to look down the street.

"Uh-huh," I said, eyebrows raised.

I saw Betsy's eyes light up, and a smile spread wide on her face as she tracked the rose and cream colored vehicle rounding the bend. I followed it as it meandered up the street to us.

When it reached us, I saw my gorgeous man at the wheel, elbow resting comfortably on the lowered window.

"Hey there, baby!" Jesse said as he hopped out of the... truck? Van? I didn't know what it was, but it was awfully cute.

"Hey there, yourself." I leaned over to give him a kiss that left me feeling warm inside. "Is this the project you've been working on? It's beautiful. Why have I never seen this one?"

"I had her way out in the back. You probably never noticed. She's beautiful, huh? She's a 1963 Divco dairy truck. Used to use these for deliveries and such back in the day."

I ran my hand along the smooth curved lines of the hood. This vehicle was *cute*. It looked like a delivery truck from the 1950s, all big curves and smooth rounded edges. It made me think of Eleanor Rose. It fit right into the period when she'd been alive. I felt a fierce longing for it. "Oh, Jesse, you should be so proud. When's the show?"

"Oh, she's not going to a show."

"Why not?" I said, surprised. "You already have a buyer? That's fantastic!"

"Something like that," he said.

His oversized hand grabbed mine, tight and warm, and he led me to the side panel. What I thought was a painted area separating the panels, I now saw was a large piece of butcher paper framed with cream colored masking tape. Jesse looked at me square in the eyes, looking sort of nervous as his hand gripped the edge of the paper.

"You know I love you, baby?"

"I do," I said. "Right back at ya." I got up on my toes and kissed him again. Jesse pulled back the paper to reveal a large Eleanor Rose Baked Goods logo painted on the side of the truck.

My hands went to my mouth and tears pooled in my eyes. "What? Me? Jess—" I couldn't speak. I couldn't find words.

He grabbed my hand again and said, "You need something better to haul all those deliveries around in. Plus, I want my truck back," he chuffed.

I threw myself at him. I mean literally jumped in his arms, wrapped my legs around his waist, and rained kisses all over his cheeks, head, and anywhere I could reach.

He laughed heartily now. "I see you like it?"

He looked in my water filled eyes as I nodded my head vigorously. It was all I could manage.

"Come on, take a look inside."

He opened the small side door, similar to those on a school bus. Max came tearing out of there and yelped and circled around me in excited yips. Steve, Michael, and Jameson poured out yelling, "Surprise!"

I was laughing and crying now, damnit.

I turned to Jesse. "Move in with me. No, wait, let's get married. I mean, I know you've been staying with me forever, but I want it to be official. You still have stuff at the apartment, and I don't like it."

I put my hand over my mouth. Did I just ask my boyfriend to marry me? I loved this man. I loved him with everything that I was, and the thought of not waking up with him in our bed each morning wasn't even an option for me at this point. This moment though, with the love in Jesse's eyes, and these friends that were now my family, it was right. It was the exact right time.

"Oh yeah. We're definitely getting married," Jesse said as he came at me.

The End

ABOUT THE AUTHOR

Helene Laval suffers from a chronic case of wanderlust, and is currently settled in the desert southwest. When she's not reading or writing, you'll find her traversing a dusty trail on horseback, struggling to hike a mountain with a five figure elevation, or hitting the road to enjoy an adventure with her family.

Visit her online at www.helenelaval.com, or any of the usual haunts below.

Printed in Dunstable, United Kingdom

68490388R00129